To Louis

I hope

book and Go Daw...



# GRIT

By Drew Mitchell

Cover designed by Bobby Rees
www.BobbyRees.com

Cover photo courtesy of
Hargrett Rare Book and Manuscript Library / University of Georgia Libraries

Although inspired by actual events, people, places, and organizations, this is a work of fiction.

First Edition: December, 2018
Independent Publisher
ISBN: 9781793234346

This book is dedicated to my wife, Tracy.
A wonderful mother to our boys
and the love of my life.

# A LETTER FROM THE AUTHOR

Georgia football has been, and always will be, an important part of my life. I graduated from UGA (University of Georgia) in 1990 and even asked my wife and fellow alum, Tracy, to marry me during the second quarter of the 1992 Homecoming game. But I was first captivated by the Bulldogs as a twelve-year-old boy during the 1980 National Championship season. I listened in awe to radio legend Larry Munson when he described how the great Herschel Walker had 'run through two men' and later begged Lindsay Scott to run. Larry didn't mean to beg Lindsay to run, but he had to.

My grandfather, Papa, took me to my first Bulldogs game in Athens the following year. He graduated from UGA in 1933 and was in attendance at the inaugural game played in Georgia's Sanford Stadium back in '29 when Yale came down South and got beat 15-0. Papa had season tickets for as long as I know and was a DGD (Damn Good Dawg) through and through.

Two days after Papa passed away, Georgia came from behind to beat Auburn on a miraculous 4th down play with just over a minute to go. During his service, my brother suggested that Papa may have secured the Lord's good graces before the snap, and I placed a red Georgia hat upon his head before we closed the casket.

Rest in peace, Papa. We love you.

Speaking of Auburn, the rivalry between the two schools is one of the most storied in all of college football and is a significant topic in this book. The series first began in 1892 and is now dubbed the 'Deep South's Oldest Rivalry.' At the time of this writing and after 123 games, the Dawgs lead the series 59-56-8 and have been victorious eleven out of the past fourteen meetings, including the SEC conference championship game in 2017.

I feel that it is important to note that Auburn University has existed under four different names since her inception. During the years that this story takes place (1896-97), it was known as the Agricultural & Mechanical College of Alabama. But for familiarity sake, I have decided to reference them as Auburn throughout the book.

In those early days, the University of Georgia was commonly referred to as 'U of G' instead of 'UGA,' and the football team was known primarily as the 'Red and Black' versus the 'Bulldogs.' I have elected to use the more historically accurate terminology in my descriptions of Georgia.

There were also subtle differences in how football was played compared to the game of today, and I made a point to take all variances into account. These involve the areas of scoring, field dimensions, and some of the basic rules (only 3 downs to make 5 yards, for example).

* * *

Despite being an avid Bulldog fan for most of my life, I wasn't introduced to the name 'Von Gammon' until the early part of this century. I was immediately hooked by the story that goes along with him and his mother Rosalind and started researching the people and events involved as best I could at a time before Google was a household name. I suppose at face value, one could assume that this is just a story about football, or more specifically about Georgia football, but it's much more than that. It's about coming of age, chasing a dream, facing adversity, dealing with tragedy, and most importantly – unconditional love.

In 2004, I began writing the first draft of a screenplay entitled, *Von Gammon.* I had gathered basic historical facts, but what I could not find were the very personal details and life stories of those involved. Therefore, I took what information I had and wove a fictional narrative that filled in the gaps between actual events on the timeline.

Over the next decade, I did my best to share my work online with the film industry, hoping that someone in the business would discover my masterpiece and greenlight it for the big screen. I once even flew from Atlanta to Los Angeles to participate in one of those 'pitch-fest' events where I sat across the table from producers and agents and gave it my old college try. Alas, none of my efforts led to anything, and I eventually gave up.

Then, in the spring of 2018, I self-published my first novel, *Mulligan,* using Amazon's online services and realized that I could adapt my screenplay into a book. And 'voila,' here we are today!

Even with the power of today's online search engines, there are still many unknowns about how those in my story lived out their lives from day to day. Therefore, while most of the characters may have been real persons, their words and actions within the story aren't necessarily so. You will find that much of what I've written is true, but I have most certainly applied creative license to tell my tale. Consider the blockbuster movie *Titanic* along similar lines – a fictional story framed around an actual event. My historical sources are credited at the end of the book.

* * *

Before you delve into Chapter One, picture this: you are entering the late 19$^{th}$ Century and dropped smack-dab in the middle of the Second Industrial Revolution. It was a time when civil men and women wore chic hats for the sole purpose of fashion while the 'brutes' that played ball on the gridiron wore nothing to guard their skulls when smashing into one another. A thick head of hair was pretty much the best protective equipment any player had at the time.

Collegiate football originated in the northeast and was initially commonplace amongst what are now Ivy League schools. Squads from Yale and Harvard met for the first time in 1875, with Harvard winning 4-0. However, Yale was victorious seventeen of the next eighteen years, fueling grave frustration among Harvard students and alumni.

The 1894 edition of 'The Game,' as the matchup has been named in more modern days, was played at a place called Hampden Park in Springfield, Massachusetts, and it was an especially ruthless contest. In all, they carried seven players off the field that day for various injuries – four of them permanently crippled.

In the weeks that followed the press had a field day of their own. They quickly dubbed the '94 match 'The Hampden Park Blood Bath,' and the majority of journalists that followed the story openly favored an outright ban of college football.

Following the game, Harvard President Charles Eliot was furious. Not because his team had lost to Yale once again, but because he felt that the game of football had no rightful place within his university curriculum. He cited its brutality and an ever-increasing number of severe injuries and sided with the journalists.

Ironically, ticket sales were on the rise. And as these northeastern programs developed massive fan bases, some of their learned football men traveled south along the eastern seaboard to teach and grow the game at other colleges and universities during the 1890s, including 'U of G.'

I hope you enjoy Von and Rosalind's story!

*"Every time a player goes out there, at least twenty people have some amount of influence on him. His mother has more influence than anyone. I know because I played, and I loved my mama."*

PAUL 'BEAR' BRYANT

# FIRST OF TEN

*My dearest Rosalind,*

*You have been the single guiding light in my life — a devoted and caring mother to our children, an exemplary female pillar in our community, and most importantly my encourager, lover, and best friend. I will miss you deeply.*

GAMMON HOUSEHOLD
WEDNESDAY, JUNE 3, 1896

Modern advancements had made it an exciting time in Rome, Georgia, located about seventy miles northwest of Atlanta in the foothills of the Appalachian Mountains. For one, Rome's very first telephone switchboard had recently been installed downtown, and wires that somehow relayed human voices from house to house were being strung throughout the city. That is, at least on the streets where families who could afford to subscribe to the new and miraculous technology resided.

The local newspaper had printed a schedule informing the townspeople when they might expect a crew of surveyors to arrive in their area and plot out the necessary plans for hanging these lines. It became a popular pastime of residents to wait for and watch the technicians do their work outside their homes.

This was no different for Rosalind Gammon; a tall, attractive woman with auburn colored hair and a beautiful smile. She was a fixture on the local social scene and served as President of the Daughters of the Confederacy, Rome Chapter. Her husband, John Aiken (J.A.), had once risen to the rank of Captain in the Confederate States Army. He had suffered some slightly debilitating injuries during the war but managed well-enough to now own a successful clothing store downtown and serve on the city council. They, along with their children, were regarded as one of Rome's prominent families.

Their house, located on Third Avenue, was a white, two-story wood-frame structure and an appropriate representation of their mid to upper-class position in the city, thanks to that reputable and thriving business on the square. The dwelling was situated just above the Rome train tracks and only one block away from the Etowah River.

Encouragers of all things sport, the Gammons had provided their sons with athletic equipment of all kinds. There were two tennis courts in the backyard and even a trapeze set-up in the barn. Barbells, boxing gloves, and balls galore were some of the accessories found around the home that were as common as window dressings. Because of the playground like atmosphere they'd created, the house had for years been a frequent gathering place for nearly all the boys in Rome.

According to the newspaper, the crew from Southern Bell Telephone was due to appear on Third Avenue sometime during the week of June 1st. Rosalind had spent most of Monday and Tuesday porch sitting while awaiting their appearance, but they never showed.

It was now a few minutes after eleven on Wednesday morning, and she'd just whipped up a pitcher of homemade lemonade. Rosalind carefully stepped over a medicine ball on her way out the door. She took a seat in one of the rocking chairs that fronted a bunch of tennis racquets propped against the wall behind her.

A wave and a smile to a passing neighbor was interrupted by the arrival of a man wearing what was clearly a working uniform. She stood and met the gentleman about halfway down the path that led from the street to her front steps.

As suspected, the man was a representative from the phone company. He introduced himself as Marty Haskins and explained that he was there to take measurements and plot positions of one or two poles that would carry the telephone line along the street in front of their home. He explained that once, or if, they subscribed to the service a separate line would be connected from a street pole to the house.

"You've got a very lovely home, Mrs.," Marty quizzed as he glanced down at his book.

"Gammon. Rosalind Burns Gammon," she returned with a polite nod. "And we most certainly plan on taking full advantage of your service, Mr. Haskins. Most of our children will be out of the house by this fall, and it will be wonderful to have the ability to speak to them from a distance. Why, I participated in a phone call down in Atlanta last year, and it was an amazing experience."

Once the pleasantries had ended, Rosalind returned to the porch and filled her glass while Marty went about his work. She sipped on her drink and watched with great interest as he inspected the distance and various angles coming from the proposed pole location in the Maddox yard next door.

After a short while, Marty summoned a colleague who had been working across and down the road, and they came together in front of the path that led to the Gammon porch. Rosalind could not hear the discussion as Marty pointed above. He shrugged and pointed some more as they evaluated the situation. Nearly five minutes passed before Marty and his consultant parted, and he made a few more notes in his book before waving to Rosalind.

Taking that as a signal to engage once again, Rosalind met him by the street, eager to hear what he had to say.

"Mrs. Gammon," the technician began, "once again let me compliment you and your husband on such a beautiful home." He cleared his throat before continuing, "And these two elm trees that you have in your front yard are quite remarkable. However, I'm afraid the branches coming from the one on the left are too far-reaching and will inhibit our ability to run a continuance of utility wire down this side of the street."

Rosalind's nostrils flared and her eyes narrowed – focusing in on the intruder's face, "Now you listen to me, Mr. Haskins." She stopped and looked off to the side to gather her thoughts before espousing, "As I said before, we are looking forward to utilizing the telephone service, but you do not have permission to do anything to my beautiful elm tree."

Her temperament waned, "In fact, if you so much as lay a finger on either of them, you'll cause me to say or do something that a proper Southern lady would normally never do. Why don't you call your associate back over here and the two of you figure out an alternative?"

Rosalind glanced over at the other technician, who had begun marking an 'X' on a tree down the street with white-wash paint. That action infuriated her even more.

She took an extra step toward Marty, and this time pointed her finger to his face, "I mean it, mister! You're not taking a saw to my elm tree!"

Marty sighed, glanced down at the page of his book, and looked back at Rosalind (whose finger remained mere inches from his face). He casually stepped back and promised that he'd consult with his partner and see what they could do.

Rosalind remained silent as Haskins headed down the street toward his colleague.

At that moment, her youngest son, Will, appeared through the front door of the house and hollered out, "I can't find my church trousers, Mama!"

Will was thirteen years old. A bright lad who had excelled in grade school and showed promising scholastic potential, but a kid still who'd not yet developed a sense of fashion. Other than Sunday mornings, his typical attire consisted of garb more suited for playing in the dirt.

And there he stood at the top of the front steps, barefoot and dressed in his undergarments. A tad embarrassed, Rosalind turned her back on the men from the phone company and tended to the problem at hand. The end-of-year school social was that afternoon, and the invitation had called for students to dress in their Sunday best.

As Rosalind approached, Will stewed, "I don't understand all this fuss over wearing this stuff. I mean, me and the other boys are gonna to end up outside anyway, and I'll surely mess up my nice clothes."

Rosalind brushed his hair with her hands, then licked a finger to wipe the side of Will's mouth. He objected to the latter and backed away quickly.

"Ewww, Mama!" he yelped.

"I'll go wet a washrag from the sink then," she offered. "But we've got to get that egg off your face."

Rosalind left and returned with the cloth, but before she could wipe him down, Will demanded, "Before you finish up you've got to promise that I won't get in trouble if I dirty up my outfit."

His mother smiled and replied, "I want you to go and have fun. Why, if you come back *without* a dirty outfit, then I will be most disappointed."

A kiss to Will's forehead followed.

* * *

Across town, Von Gammon sat atop his bicycle, rocking back and forth with anticipation. He was a sixteen-year-old athletic specimen; a handsome teen with thick brown hair parted down the middle.

Some thirty feet ahead, his friend Walter Wynn stood at the official starting point ready to begin the countdown. He was the same age as Von but of smaller stature.

"Alright, Von," he began, "once you roll off, I'll start the count. We'll confirm your time when I get down there."

"I hope not to wait at the finish for you too long, Walter."

"Ha, ha, funny. Are you ready?"

"Yeah," Von responded confidently, "a thousand feet in twenty-four seconds."

The bike pedals began to rotate as Walter started to count down from three, and Von blew past him at the equivalent count of zero.

The athlete sped down the dirt road, seemingly in record starting time. After rounding the only slight bend on the route, Von's older brother Monty came into view. Standing six-and-a-half feet tall he was known as "the Strong Man of Rome." Von also saw his father, J.A., there too, who was above average height but very skinny with straight, thin hair.

Suddenly, Von focused in on an unfamiliar object. Its shiny yellow paint and chrome fender glistened in the sunlight. J.A. propped the thing up on both wheels and smiled proudly.

As the bike raced closer, Monty shouted words of encouragement, but Von was now captivated by the stationary cycle that his father held for show and distracted from what he'd set out to accomplish.

Noticing a momentary lapse, Monty began waving his younger sibling forward and screamed at the top of his lungs. Those actions helped Von regain focus, and he composed himself for the stretch run ahead.

Faster and faster he pedaled in an attempt to make up for one or two lost seconds. But suddenly, the strain that Von had put on his aging bicycle took its toll. Forging and looking ahead, he felt something wrong with the right-side pedal. Before he could do anything about it, the piece flew out from under his foot and flipped toward the side of the road. As a result, the bike catapulted into a side spin that kicked up enough loose dirt to conceal Von inside a brown cloud.

Quick to action, Monty was by his side before the dust settled. Somehow, Von had managed to remain on two feet and avoid what had appeared to be a probable accident.

“Whoa, little brother,” Monty asserted, “breaking the fifth-mile isn’t worth dying over!”

J.A. was only a few steps behind, “Are you all right, son?”

Von assured both of them that he was fine, “Yes, Father. Not a scratch.” He stretched out all four limbs to prove his condition.

At that moment, a winded Walter arrived on the scene, “Wow, that was some finish!” He held the missing pedal in the hand of his outstretched arm, which was snatched quickly by Von.

“But I’m quite sure this dang pedal has cost me too much time!” Von asserted.

“Yeah, sorry,” Walter began, “at least ten seconds by my count.”

“And unfortunately, a few feet shy of the end line to boot,” Monty added, leading Von to punish the handlebars on his bike with a slamming of fists.

J.A. was ready to brighten the mood, “Not to worry, boy. I have something here that might change your outlook. It will certainly fix that broken pedal problem.”

Von turned his head as his father pointed toward the bicycle that he’d spotted during the ride and walked over to it with the others. It lay on its side in the dirt but still sparkled shiny and new.

“What is it?” Von asked. “Whose is it?”

“Why it’s yours, son,” J.A. beamed, “a reward of sorts for winning your race last week!”

Von was stunned by the announcement and looked at Monty for reassurance.

"Yeah, little brother, it's yours all right," Monty attested. "And hopefully it comes complete with working pedals."

Von jumped enthusiastically and hollered at Monty, "This is fantastic!"

"Tell that to Father," Monty advised, "he had it sent by railroad all the way from Ohio."

"It's the newest model from the Wright Cycle Company. They call it a Van Cleve," J.A. explained. "For some reason, I've been having bad feelings about that old bike of yours. It looks like I was almost too late with this new one. Anyway, I hope you like it."

"I love it, Father!" Von assured as he embraced J.A. "It's a very generous gift."

"We had a nice month at the store, so it was a good time for it," J.A. replied. "And you should thank your mother too when you get home. After all, she gave the final say on this one, as long as you are willing to hand down your current bike to Will. I'll have to get that pedal fixed first, of course."

Von looked over at Walter and Monty and suggested, "Why don't we give it another go? This time on the Van Cleve!"

They both nodded enthusiastically.

"Just don't be out here all day, boys," J.A. countered. Pointing at his sons, he said, "Your mother is expecting you two at the house for dinner at five o'clock, sharp. And Monty, she'd like Nellie to join us as well."

Von hopped on the bike and headed back toward the starting point with Walter running behind.

"Don't fret, Father. I'll make sure we're all there in plenty of time," Monty assured.

* * *

Now fully dressed and ready for the school function, Will headed toward the front of the house alongside his mother. Rosalind turned the knob and opened the door, and to her unpleasant surprise spotted the man with the white-wash can out front, about to apply his brush to her magnificent elm tree.

She immediately scurried back inside. Will stood scratching his head as he waited for his mother to reappear.

In less than a minute, Rosalind was back. This time carrying a shotgun in her hands and moving fast. Will dared not speak as she flew by him and barreled out the front door.

After one pronounced pump of the slide-action gun, Rosalind held the firearm high in the air and hollered toward the man with the can.

"Get your grubby paws away from my tree - NOW!" she demanded.

Startled out of his boots, the man tripped backward and dropped his container, spilling the bright wash across the grass and onto Third Avenue.

With that, prep work for phone line installation was done for the day.

* * *

After Will left for the party, the house was empty. Rosalind took advantage of the time alone to catch up on some quick house chores before beginning preparations for the evening meal. She always enjoyed having the family around their mahogany dining table – one of the largest and finest in all of Rome for sure.

As Rosalind wiped down the table, she heard the distinct sound of men's voices speaking out front. No doubt, she thought, those fellows from Southern Bell had returned; perhaps with an escort from the police department this time.

In a moment of inflamed passion, Rosalind grabbed her trusty Winchester and hurried out the front door, ready to take on whoever threatened her marvelous trees, badge or not.

"Whoa there, Mrs. Gammon," pled a fellow named Jack Pierce with hands held high in surrender mode. "I didn't mean to startle you but assure you that we come in peace," he joked.

Jack was in his early twenties and wore a derby hat and spectacles. The Gammons knew him as a college friend of Monty's. However, Rosalind was not familiar with the other gentleman that accompanied him. Nonetheless, she let her guard down and apologized for the dramatic reception before going into a detailed account of her run-in with Southern Bell.

Jack, a polished young professional from Athens, Georgia, accepted her gracious explanation and dismissed the ordeal as an understandable and honest mistake. He continued by introducing his companion, "Mrs. Gammon, might I introduce you to my friend, Coach Glenn Warner from U of G."

"It is a pleasure to meet you, sir," Rosalind offered, still blushing from her outburst and a little flustered by her actions.

Coach Warner was an attractive man who stood just over six feet and sported a square jaw, broad shoulders and thick, bushy hair. He stepped forward to extend his right arm, leading Rosalind to realize that she still gripped her weapon tightly in her hands. She let out a snort before leaning it next to one of the tennis racquets against the wall and shook Warner's hand as he and Jack cautiously made their way up the short staircase.

Nodding politely, she added, "Again, please accept my apology for such an unpleasant greeting. I imagine that you are both here to call on Monty, but he's off somewhere with his brother at the moment; most likely riding bikes down by the river."

Jack replied, "Well, Mrs. Gammon, I'd never pass up an opportunity to catch up with my old pal, but I've actually brought Coach Warner here to meet you and your husband." He paused before, "And Von." Jack glanced over at the coach before continuing, "You see, stories of Von's athletic prowess have made their way to Athens, primarily thanks to Monty, and with your blessing Coach Warner wanted an opportunity to meet your boy and see if he might be interested in auditioning for the football squad at the University this fall."

Rosalind cocked her chin, "Football? At the University?"

"Why yes, Mrs. Gammon," Warner affirmed, "are you familiar with the game?"

Rosalind had supported all things sport amongst her sons but was also aware of the recent outcries against the brutality of football, which influenced her opinion of it.

"Yes, Mr. Warner," she acknowledged, "I am familiar with the game, including the many reports of injuries that its players have suffered. My husband and I have always encouraged our sons to participate in athletics, and Von is quite an accomplished cyclist and a baseball player at high school. Last fall, he and some of the boys from the baseball nine organized the first football club at Rome High. They struggled to get eleven players to show up for each game, but still somehow managed to win all of them. There was just too much fear of injury; I suppose. Mostly among the mothers."

Warner sensed resistance, "I understand that you might have some concerns based on what's been written in the papers, but I'd contend that other sports, including cycling, can be as or more dangerous than football if not performed properly. We instruct a modern style of football at U of G with formations and tactics that are much safer than before. I also find that the game instills discipline, teamwork, and confidence in my men. And, I might add, not one boy on the team was hospitalized last season."

"I don't know, Mr. Warner,"

"Please, call me Pop," he returned.

"Pop?"

"Yes, ma'am. You see, I played football myself while a student at Cornell. I just happened to be a bit older than my teammates, so the name Pop stuck with me," he explained.

Rosalind showed a glimpse of her beautiful smile and said, "Pop it is, then. And you may call me Rosalind."

Pop grinned and nodded his head, feeling as if he'd softened the shell, "Thank you, Rosalind. I assure you that we'll teach Von and his teammates the proper fundamentals, so they play the game brilliantly and with a low risk of any serious injury."

"But can you make the same promise of the opposing team, Mr. Pop? Will they also be taught the proper fundamentals?"

Warner glanced at Jack, who smiled and said, "I can vouch for Coach Warner, Mrs. Gammon. He has an impeccable reputation and is a fine gentleman, regardless of the rigid sport that he instructs. Why, I believe that his traveling all this way to gain your blessing speaks for itself, does it not?"

"Perhaps," Rosalind replied, "but you'll also want to check with Von himself and gauge his appetite for playing football; along with his father, of course. Otherwise, this may be a moot conversation."

Both men nodded in hurried agreement.

Simultaneously and by happenstance, a caravan of sorts began to arrive. J.A. first appeared galloping up Third Avenue on his horse, followed by Monty and his wife Nellie riding comfortably in their horse-drawn carriage, albeit from the opposite direction.

Suddenly and from seemingly out of nowhere, Von sped past Monty's buggy on his Van Cleve, then up and across the front yard before coming to a quick stop at the foot of the porch stairs. He almost rode into a holly bush, which prompted a quick, verbal scoff from Rosalind.

Monty, who had now disembarked from his buggy, was a step or two in front of Nellie. He gave Jack a hearty handshake and hug, "Well, if it isn't the infamous Jack Pierce!" He made sure to introduce Jack to his wife.

"It is wonderful to meet you, Miss Nellie," Jack offered. "I know Monty is smitten with you. He's written so many sweet things about you in his letters to me. Congratulations on your recent marriage."

Nellie thanked him for the kind words before Jack focused on his tall friend, "So how 'ya doing Monty?" Jack asked with a slap on his lower back. "Are you still enjoying the glamorous life as a high school professor?"

"I am indeed," Monty answered, "and putting my education degree to the test every day!" he mused. "It may be hard for some to understand, but I find the work very rewarding; especially my efforts to improve the student physical training program."

"Your college classmates and I always knew that you would become someone important," Jack complimented.

"That's nice of you to say, Jack, but I doubt I'll ever become as important as you," Monty said with a chuckle.

After tying his horse to a hitching post by the side of the house, J.A. was the last to join but quickly reacquainted himself with Jack.

"So, everyone," Jack began as he spoke to the entire group, "I'd like to introduce you to Coach Glenn Warner from Athens."

Monty was the first to shake Warner's hand, "Ah yes, Coach Warner of the football squad. I've been keeping up with the team but sorry to admit that I haven't made any of the games since graduation."

"No worries my new friend," Warner assured, "I've only one season under my belt at Georgia so far, so you'll have plenty of chances to come out and see our club play in the future."

"Pardon me for saying, but it was a tough first season at that," Monty charged. Warner bowed like a gentleman before Monty added, "However, the papers did acknowledge a noticeable improvement in play by year's end."

"I'm glad you *both* noticed," Warner offered, "and we'll continue to work on our skills this season and hopefully post a better result. And please, call me Pop."

Monty nodded before Warner turned and stepped toward Von, who had just hopped off the seat on his bicycle, "And you must be Von," Pop concluded.

"Hello Mr. Warner," Von greeted as they shook hands. "I mean, Pop . . . how do you know my name?"

"Now *you* may still call me Coach Warner," Pop said with a smile. "I know your name because I've heard so much about your athletic promise. It is a pleasure to meet you."

Rosalind, who had been standing patiently at the top of the porch steps, suggested they move the conversation inside. But before anyone moved an inch, J.A. aggressively grabbed Pop's hand and gushed, "I for one need no introduction to you, Coach Warner."

His grin grew wide as Warner reminded to call him Pop.

"Yes, sure thing, Pop. What a pleasure."

"And it's mighty fine to meet you . . ." Warner ended in the tone of a question.

"John. John Gammon. Please call me John."

"The pleasure is all mine, John."

Noticing that his father had yet to release Warner from his grip, Monty intervened by taking J.A.'s arm and separated the two. After that, Rosalind insisted that they all come into the house for some of her pineapple sherbet. That offer spurred everyone to walk quickly up the steps and through the front door. Over time, her homemade frozen treat had become a summertime favorite of all the kids in the neighborhood.

Once inside, J.A. showed each of the men a seat in the parlor as Rosalind and Nellie disappeared to get refreshments. Some small talk about the weather and the trip over from Athens took place before J.A. got them back on track with the more important topic.

"Pop, I have to say that I love football. It is so darn exciting to watch!" expressed the elder Gammon. "And to think that the U of G trainer is sitting right here in my house – why that's some pumpkins right there!"

Jack spoke up, "Mr. Gammon, you might be interested in knowing that Pop has come to Rome to meet Von and invite him to try out for the squad this fall."

Eyes widened and lips licked as Rosalind arrived in the room carrying a tray of sherbet cups. Nellie was right behind with a coconut cake and placed it on the center table, sliced and ready to enjoy.

"Rosie, did you hear what Jack just said?" J.A. shined, "Pop wants our boy to play football at the University."

"Yes, I am aware," Rosalind returned with a half-baked smile. "And these men already know my feelings regarding the matter. I am all about Von continuing his athletic pursuits in college, but would like some assurance that his safety is of primary concern. I know how hard he goes at everything he does."

Warner cleared his throat before, "Let me clarify that even if Von is interested, there would first be a mandatory tryout period. But after hearing about his prior accomplishments and athletic ability, I am quite certain that we would find a position on the team for him, even as a freshman."

Rosalind passed by the men and offered each a dessert cup. Warner accepted one with gratitude before continuing, "As I was explaining outside to Mrs. Gammon, I ensure the squad learns and executes the latest techniques and fundamentals of the game. When the game is played correctly, we greatly reduce the chance of injury. I have found that football in the collegiate realm instills discipline and confidence in my men that ultimately leads to improved performance in the classroom. I am also convinced that it leaves a positive influence that remains with them well after graduation."

"And it is so exciting to watch, too!" chimed J.A.

Rosalind returned with a less enthusiastic tone, "I understand there may be positive attributes to playing football, Mr. Warner. But broken bones are not, and they take a long time to heal."

Warner swayed the conversation, "I've realized that we've yet to hear from the lad himself." He turned to Von, "What do you think about playing ball at the University?"

After a brief moment of reflection, Von replied, "I played some football in high school, but my interest in the game surged when Father and I traveled to Atlanta last year to see your Georgia team play the Auburn Tigers during the World's Fair. That experience took my breath away."

Everyone's attention was locked on Von as he turned toward Rosalind, "Mother, I have not told you, but Walter and I have actually discussed the possibility of pursuing football at college. Perhaps Coach Warner coming here today was meant to happen. I think I may have been called."

"Called? This is not the clergy, son."

Von stayed the course, "I know you worry about me, Mother, but I risk injury in just about everything I do. Why earlier today I almost had an accident on my bicycle, but that's not going to stop me from riding. You've got to trust that I can take care of myself."

"Hear, hear," Jack toasted as he raised a spoon full of sherbet.

"And besides," Von belted, "I'd sure like to help Pop beat those bastards from Auburn!"

"Richard Vonalbade Gammon!" Rosalind barked. "Watch your tongue!"

With a chortle, Pop interjected, "It's quite all right with me, Mrs. Gammon. Defeating Auburn is of primary concern right now. As Monty so kindly mentioned before, we may have improved last year, but the fact remains we lost that World's Fair game to them. And I admit their coach, John Heisman, outsmarted me with his tricky play calling."

"You played 'em a heck of a contest though, Coach. It was close to the end and very exciting!" J.A. encouraged.

"A game we could have and should have, won. But a loss nonetheless," Warner conceded. "I was surprised to have been given a six-dollar per week raise after that game to stay on for another season. Of course, the Georgia management said they wanted to beat Auburn, even if we lost to all the rest."

J.A. proposed, "Well, Von, I think it should be up to you to decide. Your mother will always worry about you, regardless."

Von made direct eye contact with Pop, "I want to play football for you, Coach Warner."

# GOING FOR IT

GAMMON HOUSEHOLD
LATER THAT EVENING

Von stared at his bedroom ceiling while tossing a football up and down. The secondhand of his clock ticked softly, but inside his head, the sights and sounds of the past year's World's Fair football contest played out in full color and volume.

The creaking staircase signaled approaching footsteps, and Von rolled his head in that direction just as his mother appeared through the open door.

"Von, I'm hosting a Daughter's meeting here tomorrow. Do you think you can spend the afternoon at Walter's?"

Von turned his head upward again and tossed the ball once more as if his mother had not said a word. Upon catching it, he sat up in the bed and glanced toward a magazine that sat on a side table.

"Mother, have you ever heard of a man named James Connolly?"

Rosalind began to pick up some of her son's clothes off the floor and returned, "James who? Is he from Rome?"

"No, Mother," Von answered in a slightly irritated tone, "he's not from anywhere around these parts. He won the first ever gold medal during the Olympic Games in Greece last month. He championed the hop, step, and jump competition for the United States, and I've been reading about him in my magazine."

Rosalind nodded with indifference before Von went on, "He did something great, Mother. And things didn't come easy for him, either. No matter, he made it onto the Olympic stage and won that gold medal. It says in the article that he has something called grit. What's grit, Mother?"

Rosalind broke from cleaning and set her eyes on Von, "It means determination. Fortitude. Courage, even."

Von shrugged his shoulders.

"Like when the Rebs fought at Gettysburg," Rosalind explained. "They were outnumbered and suffered more casualties than the Yanks, yet they stood their ground and fought hard for three long days; up and until the very end. General Lee may have surrendered the battle, but those men believed in their cause and never gave up, even in the most challenging circumstances. That's what grit is, son."

Von lobbed the football between hands and surmised, "Well, I'm no fighting soldier, but like James Connolly, I want to do something great in sport. I'd love for someone to write a story about me someday and tell everybody that I've got grit, too."

"Well, I don't need to read a newspaper story or anything else," Rosalind asserted, "I already know you have it."

Von smiled but said nothing, prompting Rosalind to continue, "You've already achieved so much at such a young age. Look here," she picked up one of the many trophies that lined the room and read from it, "the nation's best amateur cyclist . . . that says best in the *nation;* riding a mile in just two minutes flat!" Placing that award back she pointed to another, "And this one, the Georgia Prep High

School baseball championship. All of these are great accomplishments, sweetheart."

"Yeah, but the only people who've seen me do these things or know who I am are family and folks around here," Von sighed. "James performed in front of the entire world. Why I bet a thousand people will read about his medal in this magazine."

Rosalind sat down on the bed next to Von and pulled him close, "You can be such a dreamer, Von. I love you and will support you with whatever you set out to do, but you'll be seventeen this year and about to head off to college. And when you get there, I want you to focus on academics and start accepting the responsibilities that come with being an adult. At least promise me that you'll put as much time into your studies as you do with your games and such," she said with a wink.

After a pinch on the cheek and a flash of her loving smile, Rosalind stood and walked toward the door saying, "And you can start being responsible by coming down and helping me clean up the kitchen."

Von fell back onto his bed and promised to be down shortly, but not until he finished reading the Connolly article.

Will's voice shouted up the stairwell, "Hey, brother! Emily is outside asking for you!"

"Alright, tell her I'll be down in a 'sec!" Von answered as he jumped to his feet.

"Hold on there," Rosalind contended, "for me, it's 'Let me finish reading,' but for Emily, it's 'Down in a 'sec?'"

"Don't fret, Mother. We've got all night to clean up the kitchen, but Emily has a curfew to keep."

* * *

"It's been an incredible day, Em," Von attested. "First, Father surprised me with a brand-new bicycle, and then the head trainer from U of G comes all the way from Athens to meet me and ask if I wanted to try out for the football squad. I suppose that I'm truly blessed."

Excited for the future, Von cast his attention away from Emily and out onto the front yard, where he imagined a football scrimmage taking place right in front of him.

Emily was happy that Von was happy. But inside she felt broken. Something was changing in their new-found relationship. He'd only asked Emily to be his girl some two months prior, and now he was making plans to leave Rome to begin a new life while she would remain in town for another year of high school.

She knew that a catch like him didn't come around every day. He was probably the most-liked person in all of high school, and the fancy of just about every teenage girl in the county.

"I'm glad for you, Von," she forced with a swallow. "We'll have to make the most out of the summer together before you leave for school."

An uneasiness in Emily's tone broke through, and Von turned away from the make-believe action out front. It was dusk, and the soft light of the evening accentuated Emily's pretty face. Her long, strawberry colored hair captured a few rays of remaining sunshine and sparkled in places.

Von wanted to lean over and kiss her but held back due to his chivalrous nature. They'd only kissed a handful of times before, and always well out of view – especially parents or siblings.

He reached across his rocking chair and took her hand, "Hey, don't be sour, Em. You're my girl today, and you'll still be my girl after I leave for Athens."

"That's easy for you to say now," she challenged. "Once you start school over there and become a big star on the football field; well, all the pretty girls at the Lucy Cobb school will surely be running after you." Emily let go of Von's hand before adding, "And then you'll forget about me. I'll just become some lowly, pitiful, high school girl in your opinion. How can I possibly compete with all that affection from college girls from so far away? It's inevitable."

Von was surprised by Emily's concern and asked, "Come on, you're not serious, are you?"

She nodded with puppy-dog eyes.

"You shouldn't worry like that, Em. Why you'll be enrolled at Lucy Cobb only one year from now, and until then I'll be focused on chasing footballs, not girls."

"You should first focus on your studies if you even want to be there a year from now," she advised. Emily leaned back in her chair and propped her feet on the porch railing, herself now staring away from Von and out onto the front lawn.

It was getting darker by the second, and Von felt the need to prove his affection before his time with Emily was up.

"I want to kiss you, Em."

Her feet dropped quickly from the railing, and her neck spun toward Von to say, "Are you out of your mind? Kiss me here, on your front porch?"

After taking a moment to look around and consider the proposal further, Emily concluded, "No way. Not here. It's too risky. Your mother and father are just on the other side of that window. You know the rules."

Von stood from his chair and reached out for her hand. Following another glimpse back toward the window, Emily stood and reluctantly took his hand.

"I feel as if I need to prove my feelings for you. I want to kiss you," he said.

Again, Emily insisted that a kiss was out of the question, but Von would not stop and begged like a four-year-old.

"I've got to get home," she insisted. "It's already five minutes past my curfew. Daddy will be upset."

"Then kiss me and go," Von demanded. "You and I must not part before we show our feelings for one another."

Emily gasped as he pulled her into his chest, their lips only inches apart. Both heads swiveled as lips moved closer together.

A slight knock against the window woke Emily from her stupor. She stopped, just as their lips first touched, and nervously turned to see who or what had made the noise.

And there was Will, staring out of the glass with his hands cupped around his face and eyes as big as silver quarters.

Emily pushed back. Although unseen in the dark, her face was beet red from embarrassment. Without another look toward Von, she scurried down the porch steps and mumbled some version of "see you tomorrow."

* * *

Frustrated, Von shut the front door a bit too loudly, which distracted J.A. from his newspaper. "Von, is that you?" he cried out from his seat in the parlor.

Before he answered, Von turned toward the 'peeping Tom' who now sat on the floor by the front window. Will held his nose and quietly giggled and pointed at Von.

"I said, is that you, Von?" came again from the parlor.

Von lipped a silent threat at his brother and showed a fist before answering, "Yes, Father. It's only me."

J.A. requested that he join him so they could discuss necessary preparations for football tryouts. But before Von could make his way into the parlor, Rosalind appeared and took his arm, saying to J.A., "Hold a minute, John. You keep to your stories a bit longer while I speak with Von about something."

The elder Gammon moaned before flipping his newspaper back open.

"I promised that I would help you clean up, Mother, and I still intend on doing so. Let me tend to Father, and I'll be in there shortly."

Rosalind shook her head, "I've already done the kitchen work. I want to discuss something else with you, and it's very important that you listen and understand what I have to say."

"If it's about football you've made yourself clear about that," Von declared.

"I'm glad to hear that. But no, it's not about football. It's about Emily." Rosalind revealed.

Von shrugged his shoulders before she continued, "I know that you are smitten with her and she with you, but you are the man in the relationship, which means that it is your responsibility to control the situation when the two of you are together, especially alone. You must be cordial and respectful of her at all times."

Von sighed and tried to turn his head, but Rosalind took his chin and turned it back, "Character is defined by what you do when no one is looking. Do you understand that?"

"Aw, shucks, Mother," Von complained. "Were you peeping out the front window, too?"

Rosalind placed a finger over her lips and said, "Your father and I have raised you in a Christian home and have always taught you to act like a Southern gentleman. And until now, you have behaved like one – at least as far as I am aware."

Von shook his head over what he felt was an undeserved interrogation.

Rosalind paused until the sound of flipping newspaper pages broke the silence, "You must understand that your decisions, whether good or bad, influence our reputation. Folks respect the Gammon name across Floyd County and many parts of this state, and we'd prefer that it remain that way. And don't forget that your actions also reflect upon Emily's family as well."

"Yes, ma'am," Von conceded. "It was just gonna be one kiss. I swear it."

"Kiss?" Rosalind questioned. "What kiss?"

Von scrunched his face at Rosalind before they both broke out in a chuckle.

"And one last thing," she added, "you're about to head off to college. Are you sure it's the right time to encourage a courtship with Emily?"

“I really like her,” Von insisted. “She’s pretty and has been very nice to me. Just because we’ll be separated for most of next year doesn’t mean that we can’t still long for each other.”

Her son’s innocence touched Rosalind and she embraced him in a hug.

“Absence makes the heart grow stronger,” she whispered. “That’s what they say at least.”

# TWO-A-DAYS

NORTH ROME ATHLETIC PARK
SUNDAY, SEPTEMBER 20, 1896

After a long, hot, Georgia summer hanging out together on front porches and around watering holes, Von and Emily decided to spend a relaxing afternoon at the city park on the day before he parted for Athens.

With his back on the quilt that covered the grass beneath, Von chewed lazily on a piece of hay-straw with his eyes fixated on the clouds above. Emily sat with her legs crossed, knitting something with red yarn. A calm breeze topped off the perfect outdoor setting.

Referring to her knitting project, Emily said, "I am sorry to have not yet finished this going-away gift. This quilt we're sitting on took much longer to complete than I had expected."

Von continued to stare and chew. Chew and stare.

"So, have you decided what subjects you plan on studying during your first term?" she quizzed.

"I don't know yet."

Emily shook her head, "Classes begin on Wednesday, and you still don't know yet?"

Von waved his hand dismissively, "I reckon' if I don't pass the freshman admission exam tomorrow it won't matter anyway."

"You've been studying for it, haven't you?"

Von rolled his eyes.

"You know what; you should have started reading books months ago and learned what they're all about," Emily chastised. "You do realize that everyone in college reads the classics, don't you? All of the students will be talking about them."

"Hey, I read things," Von protested.

"Your professors will have no respect for those sporting rags of yours."

After no reply or change in his demeanor, Emily changed her tone, "How about we stop talking about school and just enjoy each other's company? After tomorrow, we probably won't see each other for at least two months. You do know that I lied and told my father that I was going over to Olivia's house today so that I could be alone with you, don't you? I even had the gumption to sneak out this picnic basket without him seeing."

Sensing her angst, Von sat up and gave Emily his full attention. But the straw was still hanging from his mouth. In one swift motion, Emily plucked it out from between his lips and threw it into the wind, which carried it some ten or twelve feet away.

"Why'd you do that, Em?" Von contended. "I don't mean to be inconsiderate; it's just that . . ."

"I know what *it* is," Emily interrupted. "Your mind is fixed on football and not me."

"Truthfully, you're only half-right," Von stated. "I'm also occupied with thoughts about my mother."

"Your mother?"

"Well, yeah," he said matter-of-factly. "Everybody is excited about the season, and I'm ready to hit the ground running. But I also promised Mother that I wouldn't get hurt. If I do, she'll likely pull me out of school and make me come back home. But what good is being on the team in the first place if I end up giving less than one-hundred percent on the field?" Von stopped before, "I only play at one speed, and that's full speed."

Emily could not hold back laughter after hearing that.

"Laugh all you want," he griped, "but it's quite the quandary!"

"That is ridiculous, Von. Mamas worry about their babies. That's what they do. You can't hold back on your game because of her."

"How about you? Are you not worried about me getting hurt?" he asked.

Emily answered, "A little, perhaps. But I'm not your mother, so probably not as much as her." She paused and looked him over, "But it does worry me that you'll be over there all alone. You could use a responsible female figure to look after you."

"And you're supposed to be the responsible female figure?"

She nodded, "Yes, and I promise to be by your side all the time once I get over there next year."

Von grinned, "Well, you'll have to be on the side*line* during ball practice and games. The field is not a safe place for a delicate flower like yourself."

The couple shared a smile before Emily dropped her needles and yarn. Within seconds, she maneuvered herself above Von and pressed him upon the quilt. This time, the kissing came without hesitation.

* * *

UNIVERSITY OF GEORGIA
MONDAY, SEPTEMBER 28, 1896

One week before, on the morning that Von had departed for Athens, Rosalind requested that he consider joining a fraternity. She hoped this would surround him with a group of students who prioritized academics and prepared for life after college, particularly a professional career. Jack Pierce had been a member of Sigma Alpha Epsilon (SAE) and offered to introduce him to the fellows there. Her parting words to Von were, "After all, you cannot earn a wage playing football, son."

Like Von, his friend Walter had enrolled at the University. They were roommates in the dorm and had been practically inseparable since arriving on campus. That remained the same on the first day of football tryouts.

The two sat inside the dimly lit athletic dressing room that was located in the basement of their dormitory, securing the last of their armor before heading to battle. With the laces on their canvas jackets pulled tight and athletic boots on, they stood to inspect one another.

Von's shoes were uncomfortable, and he sat back down to remove them.

"So, do you still plan on going over to the fraternity house tonight?" Walter inquired.

Von stretched both shoe tongues before pushing his right hand all the way up and inside the boot.

Walter waved a hand in front of his friend's face, "Hey, are you in there somewhere? I'll be fine on my own if you choose to go."

Von remained focused on his feet.

"I'd go if I were you. I bet there will be lots of pretty girls over there."

"I swear this right shoe is a size smaller than the left," Von muttered.

"Hello?" Walter said sarcastically. "The fraternity? Tonight? Girls?"

Von finally pushed his foot all the way into the right shoe and replied to Walter, "You're asking about the fraternity?"

Walter emphatically threw his arms up in the air.

"Yeah, I'll most likely go and see what they're all about," Von confirmed. "But I don't expect there to be any girls. Not tonight, anyway. It's only supposed to be an introduction between brothers and prospective members, not a party. Besides, Emily is my girl."

Walter acted surprised to hear the response about Emily, prompting Von to expound, "Why wouldn't Emily be my girl? She's pretty and sweet and cares about me. Why, she's a responsible female figure."

"A what?" Walter questioned.

Von stood once again and looked down upon his slightly shorter friend, "You heard me. A responsible female figure."

Walter shrugged, "Listen, to me – Athens is a long way from Rome. You'd best be ready, 'cause the girls over here are gonna flirt with you like flies on stink."

"Are you calling me stink?" Von joked, followed by a playful jab to Walter's arm. "After graduation next year she's going to enroll in Lucy Cobb, and we'll be back together again."

"Lucy Cobb?" Walter snorted. "Then you'll probably see her even less than you do now. I hear those girls can't even walk down the hall to the washroom without the escort of a chaperone."

"Emily and I really like each other," Von professed. "I'm sure it will all work out between us."

"Well, what about the fraternity, then?"

Von placed a hand on Walter's shoulder, "Listen, we're about to walk onto the gridiron at U of G with a chance to play football for the Red and Black. This is the best fraternity of them all."

Suddenly, another player darted up the stairs and thrust a first-floor door open wide, filling the shadowy room below with sunlight. Von and Walter followed him outside and soon came upon the red dirt field, where they observed packs of unassembled young men walking around leisurely. Von spotted two footballs in view: one being kicked and tossed amongst four boys who'd taken the shape of a square, and another that laid next to three players sitting idly on the ground just ahead of them.

"So, what are we supposed to do, Von?" Walter inquired. "It's past nine o'clock, and I don't see Coach Warner."

Von scanned the length of the field and asked, "Isn't this the most beautiful sight you have ever seen?"

Walter glanced down at the ground, "Are you serious? This field looks no better than the one behind the high school back home. It's nothing but dirt."

After making direct eye-contact with his pal, Von declared, "It's not about the dirt, Walter. It's what happens on the dirt."

Von followed with a slap to Walter's back before suggesting, "Let's go meet some of the fellas. Monty told me to look up Hatton Lovejoy. He's from Rome, also."

The two made their way to the three players who sat with the football. The trio consisted of Cow Nalley, a short, stocky, and strong fellow with wild flowing hair; Hatton Lovejoy, and Fred Price, who both sported square jaws and athletic builds.

Von broke the ice upon arrival. "Hey gents," he began, "mind if Walter and I toss that ball around while we wait for the coach?"

The three looked up as if rudely interrupted.

Cow piped up, "Team captain's in charge of the ball until Pop shows up."

"Well, alright," Von assessed, "who's the team captain and I'll ask *him*?"

Nalley spat some tobacco juice in Von's direction and stated, "I'm the captain. Name's Rufus Ben Nalley. Been on every squad here since Dr. Herty started this program five years ago."

"So, you're Cow? Cow Nalley?" Von asked in a star-struck tone.

"That's what the boys call me," Nalley affirmed. "What's your name, stump? Stump?"

Sensing hostility, Von composed himself and replied calmly, "Name's Richard Vonalbade Gammon, but the boys call *me* Von. It's a pleasure to meet you."

Unamused by the remark, Cow spat a fresh ounce of tobacco juice, this time in the vicinity of Walter, who dared not respond.

Von spoke for him, "My friend is Walter Wynn, and we're both here to audition for the team."

"You don't say," quipped Cow, who conjured up yet another lick of juice and spat toward Von's feet once again. Lovejoy and Price chuckled.

"Like I was sayin'," Cow resumed, "been here a long time and seen plenty of kids like you two come and go. You gotta be real tough to make it on this club. Ya' figure you boys are tough enough?"

Von offered, "Yeah, I'd say we're both tough enough. We've got what they call grit."

Confused by the comment, Cow glanced at Lovejoy, who explained the meaning of the word 'grit.'

Nodding his head, Cow returned his glare toward Von and inquired, "Just how do you know that you've got this . . . grit?"

"My mother told me."

All three burst out laughing. They pointed their fingers at Von and made fun of him and his mother.

"Well, I guess I'll just have to prove it to you then," Von proposed to Cow.

Hatton interjected, "You don't have to prove it to Cow. You have to prove it to Pop. Do you know who Pop Warner is?"

"I sure do," Von said confidently. "He visited my house in Rome this past summer and personally invited me to try out for the team. That's the only reason I'm here."

His statement caught the players by surprise.

Hatton spoke again, "Did you say that you're from Rome?" Von nodded, and Hatton continued, "That's where I'm from. Class of ninety-two. What did you say your name is?"

"Gammon. Von Gammon. Class of ninety-six. You must be Hatton Lovejoy."

"That's right," he acknowledged, "How did you know that?"

"Because back home they say you're the best football player around," Von proclaimed. "My brother Monty said you were responsible for the late game safety that beat Auburn a couple of years back. He said you might show me around."

Nalley and Price erupted in laughter once again. Lovejoy gave them a sharp look but said nothing. Instead, he replied to Von, "Yeah, I've known your brother since grade school. He also helped with the baseball team over here in Athens, and I believe was the University's senior class president a couple of years back. Isn't he teaching at the school in Rome now?"

"Yes, that's right," Von confirmed.

Hatton nodded with interest, "Well I'll be. Good for him."

Cow was no longer laughing and snapped at Von, "I hate to break up you all's little family reunion, here, but when you're done kissin' Lovejoy's ass maybe we can get down to some football."

Von defended, "I wasn't . . ."

But Cow cut him off, "I reckon' if Pop come to your house you must be something pretty special." He changed direction and peered at Walter, "He come to your house too, boy?"

"No sir, he didn't. Just Von's house, sir," Walter stammered.

Cow stood to address Von. Hatton and Fred followed his lead.

"Well, Pop Warner ain't gonna visit no tenderfoot frosh if he ain't got something special," Nalley asserted. "What you got that's so special, frosh?"

Von picked up the football and glanced at Cow for approval before turning toward a building that ran parallel to the field. He then punted the ball – an amazing kick that flew over and beyond the three-story structure. Afterward, Von brushed his hands while Walter stood with jaw dropped down around his chest.

"So, you can kick," Cow sarcastically conceded. "Now, who wants to show me how fast they can run and bring that ball back?"

"I will, sir!" announced Walter. He ran off before anyone could respond and quickly disappeared.

"I'll grant that kick was pretty good," Nalley said, "but we won't have to punt much. What else 'ya got?"

"I'm going to play quarterback," Von decreed.

The blunt announcement triggered a third round of laughter from the trio. Struggling for air, Fred Price managed to say, "But you're a freshman, and Pop's not going to put a freshman behind center."

"Pardon my ignorance," Von answered, "but I don't follow the logic. It seems Coach Warner would run the best able candidate at quarterback, not the oldest."

The laughter ceased as an infuriated Cow enlightened, "You don't get it, boy. You gotta earn something like that. Whether Pop come to see 'ya or not, we don't hand out no free tickets around here. Especially to some frosh like yourself."

Cow wiped the back of his hand across his mouth before adding, "And you'd better know that you're gonna get hit harder than ever this week. I will personally step on your head once or twice. Get it?"

Von responded with confidence, "Don't you worry, Captain Nalley. I'll earn my spot. Making this team means the world to me. And I'll try to keep my head from finding the underside of your foot."

Cow spat again while the others giggled.

"Make sure your feeble little friend comes back with our ball," Nalley instructed.

"You got it," Von promised. He then turned and began jogging along in Walter's footsteps.

Lovejoy hollered out, "Hey, Gammon!" As Von turned around to face him, he offered, "Good to meet you."

Von nodded back with a smile and a salute before going on his way, but the pleasantry cost Hatton a swift punch to his arm from Cow.

* * *

*I have never forgotten the day that we spontaneously hopped on that train to Athens. And over the years, you never swayed from your original reason for insisting that we take that trip – your motherly instinct sensed that Von was homesick and could use a visit from his parents. But I know the truth, darling. It was you that felt melancholy. And it was you that so desperately needed to see her son.*

UNIVERSITY OF GEORGIA
MONDAY, OCTOBER 19, 1896

After disembarking from their train near the heart of downtown Athens, Rosalind and J.A. made their way on foot toward the University campus, asking for directions to the Old College building along the way.

Old College was considered the center of campus at the University. Its sturdy brick and mortar Georgian style construction had provided office space, classrooms, housing, and a dining facility for students and faculty for nearly one-hundred years. And it's where Von and Walter currently called home.

Upon arrival at the main entry point on campus, the Gammons paused to admire what was, at the time, known as 'The Gate;' a sixteen-foot-high, cast-iron structure designed to replicate the state seal of Georgia. An arch at the top was supported by three pillars: each respectively standing for wisdom, justice, and moderation.

Once past the symbolic entrance, Rosalind quickened her pace along the pebbled path, leaving J.A. behind and struggling to keep up. Once the distance between them began to become unmanageable, J.A. spoke up from afar, "Rosalind . . . Rosie, please slow down and allow me to catch up. Your haste is unnecessary."

Rosalind took her first break and turned to address her husband, who continued to hobble slowly toward her, "It has taken us nearly the entire day to get here, and I don't intend to waste another second."

Seeing J.A. struggle, Rosalind took a deep breath and chose to wait for him – for a moment at least. He continued to tread along but warned, "I still think we should have sent word ahead so that Von knew to expect us. He might not even be in his room."

"Come along, John," Rosalind urged. "He'll be plenty surprised and delighted to see us. And the treat of a supper out on the town will be all the better."

"Oh, I'm sure he will be surprised, alright." J.A. agreed. "Delighted? Not so sure about that one."

J.A. finally caught up with his wife, and she allowed him a moments rest while assessing the situation, "Well, if he sees our visit as a bad kind of surprise, then we'll know there are problems on a larger scale. And if he reacts with pleasure, then we'll know all is well."

"I appreciate your concern, dear, however I still don't think that barging in on the boy is the right decision."

Rosalind reminded, "You heard Monty say that according to Jack, Von hasn't been back to the fraternity house in more than two weeks. I want to find out why."

"Considering the stress of preparing for the season along with a full course-load of studies, I'd say there's ample explanation why he's not gone back," J.A. surmised. "I mean, you must agree that if he has to decide whether to drop his studies or the fraternity, then the latter is the better choice."

"You didn't mention football. Why isn't dropping football and keeping the fraternity an option?"

J.A. eased the tension by pecking Rosalind's cheek with a kiss. She insisted they carry on and together arrived at the building a few minutes later. Their first observation was that the aging structure was in need of some serious maintenance and repair.

Next stop, room 207. They exited the center stairwell on the second floor and made a right toward Von's room. Several students passed them in the hall as they made their way. J.A. tipped his hat and greeted each one while Rosalind marched straight and true toward the target without distraction.

At the door, Rosalind reached for a leather strap that activated the latch, but J.A. grabbed her wrist and insisted on some level of courtesy. She reluctantly agreed and took a step back.

Four raps of J.A.'s knuckle came next, followed by a "door's open" from someone inside. He opened the door and allowed Rosalind to go ahead of him.

They entered into the right-hand side of the room. There was an open wood-burning fireplace and a closet along that side of the wall, and two beds each positioned against the front and left side. Straight across, two windows allowed an outside view of the campus grounds, with desks pushed against the wall beneath each one.

Walter turned from his seated position in front of the desk on the left to see who had entered. A hospitable smile quickly transformed into a look of confusion once he recognized the Gammons.

"Hello, Walter. Are we not who you expected?" Rosalind poked with fun.

"I wasn't really expecting anyone, ma'am, but I can say with certainty that of all people I was definitely not expecting either of you." Remembering his manners, Walter stood and shook each hand with a nod and welcomed them. He then asked if Von should be expecting them.

J.A. spoke up, "I told Mrs. Gammon that we should have sent word ahead, but she was dead set on making this visit a surprise."

"I see. Well, I'm sure he'll be surprised, alright," Walter assured.

"We're going to take Von to the restaurant in our hotel for supper and use the time to hear all about college life," J.A. explained. "You are welcome to join us if you'd like."

Too impatient to wait for a response, Rosalind got on with it, "Well, is he around?"

Walter froze momentarily, which made Rosalind somewhat suspicious. She asked for his whereabouts again.

"He . . . he's out right now," Walter stuttered, "but, but, I don't know where. If you want to wait for him here, I'm sure he'll be along shortly." He slowed to think before suggesting, "Or you can wait safely in the lobby downstairs."

"Safely?" Rosalind asked.

"Yes, ma'am. It's still pretty early. The Yahoos aren't out yet." Walter stated.

"The Yahoos?" asked J.A with a curious tilt of the head.

"Yes, sir. It's the name given to some of the residents that live in this building," Walter clarified. "It can get pretty wild around here, especially at night. That's why they've pegged this place 'Yahoo Hall'."

It was apparent to the Gammons, and particularly Rosalind, that Walter was stalling; potentially covering up something – or for somebody. That's when her questions increased in number. Ones like: did he say where he was going? When was the last time you saw him? Where would he normally be at this time of day?

Walter's vague answers were of little help. J.A. explained that time was short. They wanted to find Von before suppertime and asked if he could suggest any places around campus where they might look for him.

"You might find him at the old library building?" Walter answered in the form of a question. "Or perhaps over at the Chapel?"

After Rosalind crossed her arms and buttoned her lips, Walter retracted both suggestions and admitted that he knew nothing about Von's specific whereabouts.

But Rosalind had a possibility in mind, "How about the football field? Do you know where the team meets for practices?"

Walter looked straight down at the floor and shuffled his feet. Rosalind knew she'd pressed the right button.

"So, he's at practice."

Walter looked up but was not quick to speak. Rosalind shrugged her shoulders waiting for an answer.

"I reckon' he might be," Walter slipped softly.

J.A. broke out in a jovial tone, "Well, why didn't you just come out and say so, Walter?" He glanced over at Rosalind and added, "You don't have to hide that from us. We are fully aware that he is on the team, you know."

That said, J.A. realized that if Von was at practice, then Walter should be at practice and inquired about it.

Walter blushed and admitted that he did not make the final roster. The Gammons began to apologize until he stopped them mid-sentence, "Thank you, but no need for that. I'm actually glad that I didn't make the team."

"Oh yeah? Do tell," Rosalind requested.

Walter realized that he was going down a path that he would probably regret and tried to change the subject. He blurted out something about his ancient language studies and pointed toward his desk.

"There's something you're not telling us, Walter," Rosalind accused. "Why are you glad to have not made the squad?"

During their conversation, the Gammons had slowly moved closer and closer toward him, and Walter found himself cornered in his own room. With nowhere to go, he confessed what he knew.

Over the next five minutes, the Gammons learned that Von and the team practiced every day, except Sundays. But the heavier news was that so far, Von had missed some classes and even failed to turn in his first written assignment in English. When asked about the fraternity, Walter revealed that Von had no plans to join because he didn't have enough time outside of football.

After unloading all of his friend's confidences, Walter felt incredibly guilty, "I'm only telling you all of this because I am a little concerned about him and don't know what to do. But please don't let him know that I said anything," he begged.

"Don't feel ashamed for telling us these things, Walter," Rosalind comforted. "It's in Von's best interest for us to know. Just tell me how to get to the ball field, and we'll forget that we saw you."

* * *

By the time Rosalind and J.A. made it over to the field, shadows coming from the trees stretched from one end to the other and cool evening temps had settled in.

They approached as a handful of boys were on the turf running a football play and kicking up dust. J.A. watched the action in front of him while Rosalind surveyed the surroundings. Among the many bystanders, she spotted three pretty college-aged girls sitting near the athletic equipment on the opposite side. Two were talking and laughing with each other while the third had her eyes on the team.

Rosalind found herself drawn to girl number three for some reason; perhaps because her auburn hair was a similar color to her own. It was cut a little shorter than the other girls, but her bangs hung low and almost touched her eyebrows. Rays from the setting sun illuminated her striking green eyes, making them visible from a distance.

J.A. brought Rosalind back from her stupor when he unwittingly slapped her arm with the back of his hand at the end of the play.

"Goodness, gracious, Ma! Did you see our boy run with that ball?!" he shouted excitedly.

Out on the field, Von was rising from underneath a pile of teammates with a football tucked under his arm. Rosalind grabbed her husband's wrist and started to pull him away from his spot, but he resisted and won his wrist back.

"Wait a minute, Rosie," he argued. "Since we've come all this way can't we at least take in a scrimmage or two more? It's gonna be dark in a bit, and they'll have to quit, anyway."

"Look around, John," Rosalind ordered. "Do you see any trainers out here?"

He scanned the area and shrugged.

"The answer is no. This appears to be an unsupervised and unauthorized session if you ask me."

"Don't you think you might be overreacting a bit? There's nothing wrong with these boys getting together for a little evening practice." J.A. contended.

She begged to differ, "There is when studies suffer as a result. Like I've told you boys all my life, I'm all for athletics until they take precedence over academics. Especially in college."

"All I'm saying is that it's not illegal to play a little football," J.A. sniveled.

Another play began on the field with Von assuming the quarterback position. He took the snap and carried the ball up the middle for a short gain before being tackled.

Furious, Rosalind left J.A. and huffed her way across the field, stirring up her some dust of her own as she hurried toward the players.

Von huddled with his teammates to discuss the next formation, unknowing that Rosalind was zeroing in from behind. In an instant, she took his right ear and began pulling him away from the group.

"Ow! Ow! Ow!" Von yelped. He was caught completely off guard and in a little disbelief once identifying his captor, "Mother? Let me go!"

Rosalind did not obey Von's directive, and those on the team laughed at his predicament. He squirmed in an unsuccessful effort to escape her grasp.

"Mother!" Von repeated, "you're hurting *and* embarrassing me!"

While spinning in her clutches, Von caught sight of the three girls, and they were also noticeably amused by his plight. He finally managed to shake loose of his mother's stronghold.

"What is wrong with you?!" he charged.

Von glanced over at the girls again, whose giggling had now escalated into fits of all-out hysterical laughter. At least that's the way it looked to Von. In a moment of fury, he spiked the ball and turned his back on Rosalind and everyone else to gather his composure. A few teasing catcalls came from his teammates.

J.A. arrived at the spot, "Let's take this conversation private, Ma."

"Why? So we don't embarrass Von in front of those girls over there?" Rosalind asked sarcastically. "Or these boys?"

Von wasn't the only one who was annoyed. Rosalind first steered her aggravation toward the pack of girls, "What are you three gals doing here anyway? Don't you have studies to tend to?"

The girls paused to look at one another, but they all just started snickering again.

Rosalind then turned her questioning on the team, "And how about all you fellas? I don't see any trainers out here, so I'm guessing this is what's called an unapproved practice session? Are there any limits on the time you spend playing games versus your school work?"

Hatton stepped forward and spoke up, "Excuse me, ma'am, but your son was named our starting quarterback today. That's quite an honor, especially for a freshman."

J.A. piped up, "*My* boy is the quarterback? Really?"

Von was accosted from behind once again, this time by his father, who despite physical limitations picked him up a few inches off the ground in a bear hug. This time, Von did not object to the physical assault.

"I knew you would do it!" J.A. shouted. He held Von's shoulders and exclaimed, "I've had dreams of you playing the quarterback position. I just knew they'd come true!"

Rosalind threw her arms up in the air and barked, "Stop this foolishness, John! Korterback or not it makes no difference if he doesn't return for his sophomore year!"

"Of course, Ma." J.A. complied and released his boy.

"Mrs. Gammon, if I may," Hatton interjected.

"Who are you and why are you interrupting this family conversation?" she asked sharply.

"My name is Hatton Lovejoy. I'm also from Rome and, it so happens, a friend of Monty."

"Is that so?" Rosalind queried.

"Yes, ma'am," he affirmed. "I think you'd be proud of your boy. He tries hard out here and that inspires us all to play harder. He's a good kid."

Cow peered over and rolled his eyes at Fred Price.

Rosalind challenged, "Harder or longer, Mr. Lovejoy? In my opinion, your team trainers already require too much time away from your books, and now you are all here wasting more time on your own accord. When is enough, enough?"

"On the contrary, Mrs. Gammon," Hatton politely debated, "being on the team has always motivated me to do well in school so I can return and play the next season. I'll let the others do their own talking, but I'd imagine they will say the same."

Von decided to speak for himself, "Mother, I have been spending more time studying of late. We don't scrimmage at all on Sundays, and this is the first weekday afternoon that we've stayed out here this late. We're just running short on time to perfect all the plays before our first game this Saturday."

"And why haven't you also made time for the fraternity?" she quizzed.

Von moved closer to his mother, "I've been to the fraternity house several times, and for the most part they're a swell bunch of fellas. But you might want to know that some of those boys are not all about academia, either. I've seen booze being drunk over there, and on some days, girls hang around late into the evening. You've got to trust that I'll make the right decisions, including what I do with my time and who I spend it with."

Grasping at straws, Rosalind nodded toward the three girls, "What about those girls hanging around *here*?"

"What about them?" Von asked. "This is public property. We can't stop them or any of these other people from watching us practice. Lots of people do it. Football is a big deal around here."

Warily, J.A. took his wife's hand and said, "It sounds like Von has been acting quite responsibly after all, Ma. Let's get him cleaned up and treat him and Walter to some supper on the town."

"No thank you, Father." Von declined. "I've got a study group an hour from now, so I'll pass on supper. But if you'd like to start this visit over tomorrow morning, I'll be in my room until I leave for my ten o'clock class."

With all the momentum from practice now lost, Cow announced that it was over for the day and the boys on the team began walking off in different directions. There was no day or time mentioned for the next session.

The three Gammons walked together in the direction of Old College. As they stepped off the dirt field and onto a grassy bank, Rosalind stopped and pulled something from the inside of her coat. She placed and held it in the palms of Von's hands. It was something like a pin cushion made of red yarn and in the shape of a heart, about four inches in diameter with 'Von & Emily' scripted in black lettering on the front.

While holding the gift in her son's hands, Rosalind said, "She asked that we bring this to you today. Emily is a sweet girl."

Von nodded in agreement and hugged his mother. J.A. gave him a hard, loving slap on the back. They shared a few more parting words before the Gammons headed off toward town to find their hotel for the night.

As they walked away, Von turned toward the spot where the girls had been. Two of them had moved on, but the girl with the auburn hair remained. From across the field, she smiled at him with her captivating eyes.

A bit flustered, Von quickly peered down at his gift from Emily, which he clutched tightly in his hands. He soon swiveled his head back toward the girl and returned a smile of his own.

* * *

A few dying embers in the fireplace cast a soft glow of light across the room. Mondays were typically one of the quieter nights of the week in 'Yahoo Hall,' allowing Von to catch up on some much-needed sleep.

But the stillness did nothing to calm Walter, who tossed from side-to-side atop his dormitory issued mattress.

"Von, are you asleep?" he asked. After waiting for what seemed to be an ample amount of time with no response, Walter sat up and rephrased his question, "Von, are you awake?"

Von turned his head toward his roommate, "I was asleep but now awake, so yes to both questions. What is so important?"

"I can't sleep because I know I got you in trouble today with your folks," he admitted. "I know it was not my place to say anything, and even tried to lie, but I eventually folded like a tent and gave you up."

"Are you kidding me, Walter? When my mother sets her mind on doing something, she's going to do it. So, whether my whereabouts came from you or someone else, she would have found me, regardless. I don't find you at fault for anything."

"Well, I know you've been under a lot of stress trying to make your mark on the team and starting school and all that," Walter stated, "so the last thing I wanted to do was make it all worse."

Outside, the nearby sound of a glass bottle skidding down a sidewalk broke the silence, followed by the snickers of a few people that echoed in the night.

From his seated position, Walter looked out the second-floor window and fixed his eyes upon the moon, "I thought we'd hear the

Yahoos out at some point tonight. It's been way too quiet, even for a Monday."

Von rolled onto his side with his face toward the wall, "Let's do our part and hush up, then. You shouldn't lose any sleep worrying about me."

Out of his friend's line of sight, Walter nodded and lay back down.

The last thing either of them heard before the brick came crashing through the window were more laughs from ground level. The projectile tumbled across the floor and came to rest in the middle of the room, surrounded by hundreds of sharp glass pieces.

Walter yelped and was up on his knees in seconds. Von raised a bit slower and positioned his legs off the side of the mattress.

"Don't step onto the floor, Walter. There is glass all over the place, and we won't be able to see all of the pieces in the dark."

The roommates heard roused voices and scurrying footsteps outside. Von wanted to eye the perpetrators and tip-toed quickly around the glass pieces, most of which were illuminated by the moonlight. He arrived at the window in time to catch a glimpse of the three boys who were running away from the scene.

"Who is it?" Walter asked from his spot on the bed.

He only had a view of their assailants' backsides, but from his experience playing behind the offensive line, he knew two of them well enough. Von took in a deep breath before he felt the pain coming from his heel. One of those glass shards had bitten him and blood was flowing.

"Did you see who it was?"

The badgering questions and the cut on his heel irritated Von, but he held his emotions in check while retrieving a hankie from his desk drawer to help slow the bleed.

Another question came, “Are you all right, Von?”

Once seated in his desk chair, Von addressed his friend, “They were running away so I couldn’t make them out very well.”

Walter started naming his list of suspects, but Von tuned him out. As he gazed out the window, he could feel his pulse through the tightly held handkerchief.

Sleep did not come easy for Von that night. Not only did it seem as if his mother had turned against him, but also his teammates. Even his close buddy Walter gave him up.

But solace came later when thinking of Emily. He determined that she was the one person who still had his back. That was his final conscious thought before entering dreamland.

# GAMEDAY

BRISBANE PARK, ATLANTA, GA
SATURDAY, OCTOBER 31, 1896

In 1896, the majority of what were considered the preeminent collegiate football programs were located in the northeastern United States. The game had been expanding southward along the eastern seaboard in recent years but comparatively speaking, still in its infancy.

A few southern upstarts, including the universities of Virginia and North Carolina, had begun making a name for themselves for their accomplishments on the gridiron, but no school south of the Mason Dixon Line was considered to be in the same league with their northern counterparts.

That said, there was a regional competition underway in the South; a race to see which college would rise to prominence and perhaps challenge the likes of Princeton, Harvard, or Yale, someday. On October 31st, U of G was ready to make a statement against North Carolina.

This was only the fifth season of play for the Red and Black compared to eight for the Tar Heels of North Carolina. The experience factor alone meant that Carolina was favored to win.

Underdog or not, the Georgia faithful were pining for a breakout victory.

Just one year earlier, the teams ended up playing twice in the same season; in back-to-back weeks, no less. That was highly unusual, even for those days. After the controversial first game, the Carolinians admitted to scoring the only points of the match on a play that had relied on a successful forward pass of the football. But passing the ball was not permitted by the rules (and wouldn't be until 1906). In a display of good sportsmanship, Carolina offered to line up against Georgia again the following week. They went on to win another close one but this time fair and square. At least that is how it was reported.

Now, after waiting a year for revenge, Georgia felt ready for another shot at defeating their new rival. With Von Gammon directing the offense at quarterback, the Red and Black had opened the season a week prior by traveling to South Carolina and soundly defeating Wofford College 26-0, a school located in Spartanburg. U of G had played well in all facets of the game, which gave her supporters much hope for an upset victory.

But the Tar Heels were also very good and off to a solid start. They entered the contest having already played three games and sported a record of two wins, no losses, and a tie (2-0-1). Impressively, they had surrendered only one touchdown during those games.

The venue, Brisbane Park, was used primarily as the home field of the Atlanta Crackers professional baseball team, but also hosted numerous football games in the fall. On occasion, U of G used both Brisbane and another called Piedmont Park, also located in Atlanta, for its higher profile 'home' games since the existing facilities in

Athens could not support large crowds. And this matchup was certainly expected to draw a large crowd.

Originally built for baseball, the site had grandstands constructed in two wings that flanked the first and third base lines with home plate in the center. For football contests, one of the goal lines ran in front of what would normally be the third base line. The rest of the field was stretched into its long, rectangular shape by going in the direction of baseball's right-field. A covered seat in the grandstand was nice, and cost more money, but some of the best viewing spots for football were left for those with 'standing room only' passes at ground level.

Von's family and close friends had agreed to meet at Brisbane and watch the contest together. Monty had secured enough tickets in the seats behind the north goalpost for himself, Nellie, J.A, Rosalind, Will, Emily, and Walter. Everyone except Walter had come in from Rome early that morning and were now in line waiting for entry through the main gate. The group moved slowly forward, albeit anxiously, and tried to keep an eye out for Walter in the crowd. He was traveling from Athens and due to arrive any minute.

The Gammon clan came upon a boy peddling some game literature.

"Come on up, folks!" hollered the street-side vendor. "Pick up your official souvenir scorecard here! Just three cents for the complete rosters of Georgia and the more powerful club from Carolina!"

Monty was offended and whined to J.A., "Did you hear that, Father? Our squad gets no respect, even in Atlanta!" Despite his immediate personal dislike for the seller, Monty paid the money and collected his card.

"Don't listen to him, Monty," J.A. contended. "Why, he can't be more than eleven years old. What does he know?"

"Yeah, I'm older than that, and I don't know *anything* about it," Will decreed.

"Well, he apparently didn't get wind of last week's romping of Wofford," Monty fussed. "And Will, you'll get a first-class introduction to football today!"

From out of nowhere, Walter appeared on the scene and shouted, "You said it, Mr. Gammon!"

Everyone was happy to see Von's best friend and took the time to greet him. It was a welcome that included a few slaps on the back and a hug or two.

"It's great to see you, Walter," said Monty, who then insisted that he call him 'Monty' and not 'Mr. Gammon.' "Save that one for my father," he kidded.

Having been the only one in the group that had not embraced or smacked him, Emily smiled at Walter and said hello in what was almost a whisper. He nodded back with a tip of his fashionable derby hat.

"So how are you and my little brother getting along as roommates?" Monty inquired.

"I couldn't ask for a better one, Mr. Monty," Walter assured.

Unable to hold back, Rosalind quizzed, "And is he spending enough time with his studies? Does he make up his bed each day?"

"You'd be proud of him, Mrs. Gammon," Walter replied. "Now that the pressure of making the team and getting ready for the season has passed, he is much more focused on his schoolwork. I can tell that he is less stressed because his spirits have been much higher of late."

"And his bed?" she repeated.

"With all due respect, Mrs. Gammon, I already got my friend in trouble once, so I'll decline comment on that one," he answered with a chuckle. "But I'd love to talk about the game today!"

That provoked a bit of laughter from all before J.A. declared, "I'm glad that you are here to help to support the team, Walter. It will be so exciting to watch them play!"

Monty held up the back of the souvenir scorecard and enthusiastically pointed to a name, "Here he is in print; Von Gammon from Rome, Georgia!"

"There's been a lot of controversy over Pop's decision to start a freshman at quarterback," Walter informed, "but he sure proved himself last week!"

"Sounds like he played doubly-darn well," J.A. followed. "I'm sorry that we didn't make the trip for that one, but it was a long way just to attend a football game."

After spending time surveying the scenery versus participating in the conversation, Rosalind eventually piped up, "John, I cannot believe how many people are here." She looked him in the eyes, "If you listen to all the politicians and college administrators lately, you'd believe that everyone is against the game of football being played at all."

"Well, I'd say by the number of people here today, there are plenty who are all for it," J.A. contested. "I read that they were expecting upwards of three-thousand spectators at this game. We are in the age of modern-day college football, Ma, and it has turned your boy into a celebrity of sorts."

"Celebrity?" Emily questioned. "I for one don't understand the fascination over boys chasing a ball around in the mud."

Monty was quick to respond, "Oh, we are fascinated, all right. And many others are, too. This game has been hyped up in the papers for weeks! It was moved here to Atlanta only because the field in Athens couldn't hold everyone that wanted a ticket."

At that moment, the line made a significant push forward, and they all stepped in front of the entryway; allowing their first full view of the field.

"Well, that's odd," Rosalind stated.

"What's that, dear?" asked J.A.

"Look at the field, John. I could swear that it slopes from one end to the other. Seems a strange way to design a surface for football games."

With heads simultaneously tilted, they all examined the field.

"It will certainly put a strain on the offenses to move uphill," J.A. evaluated. "Too bad they couldn't find a level playing field to play on."

"I guess we'll have to take the good with the bad. This place wasn't designed with football in mind," Monty informed, "but at least it's large enough to hold all these people."

One by one they handed their tickets over to the attendant before entering the grounds. They had arrived in time to see both teams run out from opposite sides of the grandstands and head to opposing sidelines.

* * *

The Gammon party made their way to the stands and into their seats just before the opening kickoff. From left to right they sat: Will, Rosalind, J.A., Monty, Nellie, Emily, and Walter amongst thousands of others. The U of G crowd was in the majority, and most wore outfits colored red or at least donned an accessory such as a scarf, etc., to identify the team they supported. Scattered throughout were pockets of folks dressed in light blue and white in support of Carolina.

While taking in the breadth of the scene, Monty recognized a gentleman named Thomas Reed on the Georgia sideline, who was a well-known University graduate. Reed carried a long stick, complete with red and black ribbons shooting out of its top end. To the enjoyment of Georgia followers, he marched up and down the U of G side of the field, waving his stick with great pride and enthusiasm.

Monty leaned to his wife, pointed at Reed and explained, "See that man with the flailing stick?"

She nodded.

"That's Thomas Reed," he continued. "One hell of a Georgia man, right there. If I remember correctly, he's from the class of eighty-eight, and I'd wager has more school spirit than a whole pack of alums put together."

Both teams had assumed positions for the kick. Everyone in the stands took to their feet to applaud and cheer, cutting Monty's commentary short.

One of the referees signaled to start the ball game.

* * *

The game had progressed mid-way through the first half with both teams having scored one touchdown apiece. On 3rd down, North Carolina lined up to punt with Hatton Lovejoy of Georgia set to return.

The Tar Heel kicker delivered a booming shot, much longer than Lovejoy expected. The ball sent him scampering backward to try and catch it. Unfortunately, Hatton's effort came up an inch or two short and the ball glanced off his fingertips and bounced behind Georgia's goal line.

After a furious rush to the football by both teams, a North Carolina player won the chase and came up with it for a touchdown. Tar Heel players, coaches, and those dressed in blue erupted.

The play had finished on the end of the field directly in front of the Gammons, allowing a full view of the fiasco. They, along with thousands of other Red and Black supporters, were stunned by the outcome. The initial shock first led to their complete silence, but the quiet was quickly replaced by a chorus of ever-intensifying jeers from the stands.

However, there was one who showed no emotion whatsoever, and that was Emily. Noticing her indifference, Walter tapped her shoulder and, because of the noise, spoke directly into her ear to explain what unfortunate thing had happened.

The catcalls and boos continued to shower down onto the Georgia sideline and Coach Warner. Pop slapped his cap against his thigh in frustration. Thomas Reed had fallen to his knees, his face cradled by both hands and prancing stick on the ground by his side.

Following Carolina's points after touchdown conversion play, Warner engaged Hatton as he returned to the sideline, "Well, Lovejoy," he began while waggling his finger, "you have certainly played hell, here!"

Lovejoy was noticeably embarrassed, and Pop swiveled his head toward all of the players that surrounded him and announced, "Next defense, I want Gammon playing in the hind position!"

By this time, Reed was back on his feet and had moved just behind the coach. "But that's madness, Pop," he asserted.

Warner spun around to face the unexpected critic.

"No quarterback that I know of has ever moved to play in the defensive rear," Reed argued.

"Well then, we will make history today!" Warner exclaimed before turning to Hatton, "Won't we, Lovejoy?"

* * *

Inspired by their impassioned coach, the team from Athens managed to score two touchdowns and take an eight-point lead by intermission.

The October sun began to hang as the second half began. J.A. noticed the oncoming darkness and complained that the game had started too late in the afternoon for the time of year. He was concerned that any action around the opposite end of the field would be difficult to see in diminishing light.

A little more than halfway into the period, the Red and Black blocked a punt deep in Carolina territory. The play gave Georgia the ball on the Tar Heel 5-yard line with a terrific opportunity to increase their lead. Fortunately for J.A. and the rest of those in the stands, this had occurred on their end of the field.

On the next snap, Von received the ball from center and handed it off to Lovejoy, who sprinted around the end of the line for a quick and easy touchdown. The score put Georgia up by 14 points, and the crowd cheered and hollered with great fervor.

In the midst of the resulting chaos, Von calmly picked up the football and looked up into the stands to find his mother. After a quick search, mother and son made eye-contact. She beamed with pride, and Von kissed the ball and lifted it in her direction along with a big smile of his own. The sweet moment was short lived as Von was quickly smothered by a herd of oncoming teammates who swallowed him up in celebration.

* * *

As the sun dipped below the treetops, Carolina scored a late touchdown and conversion kick that pulled the score closer at 24-16. However, the Tar Heels needed at least two more scores, and it was getting dark.

Before North Carolina could line up and kickoff, the officials halted play and assembled at mid-field.

Still twirling his stick proudly in the air, Reed pranced up to Coach Warner and asked what was happening.

"I'm not sure yet, Thomas," the coach replied. "It may have something to do with the poor light."

The officials broke their huddle and signaled to both sidelines. Reed pointed his stick in their direction and informed Pop that he was being called out for a conference. The crowd hushed with anticipation as Warner and Carolina Coach Gordon Johnston met with the referees.

Within moments, the two coaches shook hands and exchanged pleasantries before parting ways. Pop turned toward the grandstands and raised his arms in the air, leading the partisan crowd to break out in cheers that were so intense some folks reported hearing them from several blocks away.

By the time Warner returned to the sideline, the team was already celebrating with many of the fans who'd stood at ground level throughout the game. Others came pouring out of the grandstands.

As the stands cleared, Pop looked up in time to notice a familiar face walking toward the exit. He discreetly grabbed Von and pulled him away from the masses.

"Fantastic play and leadership out there today, young man," he began. "Way to bring us back to victory!"

"Thanks, Coach," Von offered, "but it was a whole team effort."

Turning his attention back on the man in the grandstands, Pop pointed at him and alerted Von, "You see that gent up there with the mustache and round spectacles?

Von affirmed with a nod of his head.

"That's Coach Heisman of Auburn. He is the one I mentioned when I visited your home."

"Yes, I remember. The World's Fair story," Von acknowledged.

"I'm not surprised that he came here to watch us play before this year's match. Scouting opponents before games is just another page in his playbook," Warner revealed. "I suppose he wanted to see how you have improved our offense. You ought to know they've got a nifty quarterback of their own. His name is Reynolds Tichenor. He's small as a flea, so they like to call him 'Tick'."

"I'm sure Heisman came to see the entire team play and not just me, Coach."

Placing a hand on the back of Von's head, Warner looked him dead in the eye, "You're right, kid. And he saw an awfully good team at that!"

* * *

On the streets outside of Brisbane, the natural shine of the moon and a few gas-powered pole lights fought off the darkness of night. Except J.A., the Gammon ensemble waited patiently for Von to emerge, each one anxious to see him after the big win.

Following what felt like a long time, members of the Red and Black squad began funneling out of the park, with Von near the end of the line. His face lit up with joy upon seeing everyone.

Walter was the first to approach, "Great game, Von!" he exclaimed while grasping one of Von's shoulders. "You're the best!"

Emily separated the two roommates and embraced Von with a loving hug. Next up was Rosalind, who placed her hand on Von's left cheek before kissing his right. Monty and Nellie both congratulated him on a well-played contest. Will just smiled and stared in awe at his bigger-than-life brother.

"Despite all my fussing I *am* proud of you, son," Rosalind stated.

Von thanked her and asked where his father was.

"He's trying to fetch a carriage that will take us to the train station. We'll have to move quickly or else look for a hotel room soon."

"I'm really glad that you all made an effort to come see us play," Von said to the group.

"I just wish we had time to spend together," Emily testified.

They shared another hug before Von retrieved the heart that she'd knitted for him from his coat pocket, "I've wanted to thank you for this, Em. It helps me think of you, so I carry it with me pretty much everywhere I go, even the ball games. And after today it's officially my good luck charm."

Monty changed the mood when reminding everyone of the time, "We'd better go find Father. The last train pulls out in less than an hour."

Rosalind agreed and shooed everyone away, "Right you are, Monty. You all go ahead, and I'll be right behind."

Each said their last goodbye and walked away one by one, soon leaving Rosalind alone with Von.

"Walter mentioned that your school work has improved," she confided. "I'm happy that you found a way to balance athletics and academics. Perhaps when the season is over, you can revisit the idea of fraternity."

Von returned a half-hearted expression, the kind that mothers notice.

"Von?" she said in an inquisitive tone.

Von avoided looking directly at his mother, which escalated her concern.

"Tell me what's bothering you, son."

He took in a deep breath and let it out, "I wanted to discuss my schoolwork with you, Mother, but until this moment I haven't had the chance."

Another "Von?"

"Alright, already. Geesh." He delayed. "I missed turning in another reading paper . . ."

Before he could continue, Rosalind went into defense mode and barked, "Missed another paper?! That's your second one!" She paused before concluding, "Or perhaps better said, the second one that I know about. When are you going to get your priorities in order, Richard?"

For the most part, Von didn't mind it when people called him by his first name but despised when his mother did.

Rosalind continued, "I am not fooling around with you, son. Football celebrity or not, you were first and foremost sent to the University to get an education. We've been through this before."

"Celebrity?" Von mumbled.

"Your father . . ." She paused before, "After adding up books, tuition, boarding costs, and other expenses, your father is investing about two-hundred and fifty dollars for you to attend school this year. If any one of your grades is unsatisfactory come December, I swear I'll bring you home and you can work in the store until every penny has been repaid. Do you understand me?"

Still contemplating the celebrity comment, Von was slow to reply, but did in short order, "Please calm down, Mother. I finished that paper. I just forgot to turn it in yesterday when it was due. I'll explain to the professor that I got distracted because of the game today."

"If your professors are anything like I would expect them to be, they aren't going to give a hill of beans about football and will not accept that as an excuse," Rosalind argued. "You'd be best suited to come up with a better reason than that. But don't you lie about it, either!"

An unidentified figure startled Von and Rosalind when he appeared from out of the shadows and walked up within a few feet.

"Pardon me, both of you," the man offered. "My name is Harry Hodgson. I'm a U of G alum, class of ninety-three, and a reporter for the Atlanta Constitution."

"A newspaper reporter?" asked Von.

Harry shook his head in the affirmative, “Yes, that’s right, and I cover the football games for the paper. I’ve gotta say, I was impressed by your play out there, young Gammon, and would like to get a few quotes from you for tomorrow’s story.”

Rosalind soured the moment, “I’m sorry, Mr. Hodgson, but that won’t be permissible. I’m Von’s mother, and we have a train to catch.”

“But won’t Von be on the team train?” Harry asked. “That snake doesn’t pull out for at least another hour or more.”

“Please excuse us for now. Von and I are having a family discussion,” Rosalind clarified. “I don’t want to be cross, but you’ll have to write your story without any commentary from my son.”

“Mrs. Gammon, I am not certain what concerns you, but . . .”

“Listen, mister,” Rosalind snapped, “my son is not this celebrity you all want to make him out to be. He is first and foremost a college student, and there’s no need for his quote in your paper. You should leave him be, along with all the other boys on the team, and write your stories from the sideline.”

Harry conceded, “As you wish, Mrs. Gammon. Like you I do not want to sound cross either, but I’d suggest that you not try and keep your boy under a rock much longer. He has a special gift and the world will want to get to know him better, whether you approve or not.”

Angered even more, Rosalind peered into the reporter’s eyes and fired back, “I will keep him under my rock as long as I deem necessary, Mr. Hodgson. I’ve allowed him to play this silly game to fancy all of you. Isn’t that enough?”

Harry tapped his pencil on his notepad but said nothing in return.

“Good night then, Mr. Hodgson,” she finished.

Acting on cue, Harry turned and disappeared back into the night whence he came.

Embarrassed and disappointed by his mother's behavior, Von stormed off in the direction of the team train without saying farewell.

However, Rosalind had some parting words for Von. He tried to ignore her but heard them loud and clear, "I meant what I said, son. You'll be back at home by January if you don't make your grades!"

# UNDEFEATED

ATHLETIC FIELD, UNIVERSITY OF GEORGIA
FRIDAY, NOVEMBER 20, 1896

On November 9$^{th}$, the Red and Black had chalked up their third 'W' of the year with a 26-0 victory at home versus The University of the South, a school located in Sewanee, Tennessee, that was soon destined to become one of the powerhouses of the region. That left Auburn up next on the schedule, and most of the month to prepare for the Thanksgiving Day clash.

Determined to defeat Auburn and their coach, John Heisman, Pop used that time to work his team harder and longer than usual. They put in so many hours with Warner that none stuck around for any of those late afternoon, unsupervised practices that the boys had enjoyed so much.

But with six days remaining before the final and most important game of the season, Pop decided to give his men a break. He shortened the Friday session and focused only on conditioning with no hitting. He wanted his men to have something left for the enemy, after all.

Nalley, Price, and Lovejoy lay next to one another with their backs on the ground, exercising their legs as if riding bicycles upside down. Other players ran sprints or tossed a medicine ball to stay active. Pop circled the field telling everyone several times that physical endurance would give them an advantage against their rival.

As Warner made his way over to Nalley, a freshman student named Theo caught up with him. Theo had volunteered to manage the team's equipment during the season, and for the most part, keeping an eye on their two footballs was his number one job.

"Coach Warner, Mr. Hodgson from the paper is here to see you. He said that you are expecting him."

Pop nodded, "Thank you, Theo. Tell Harry that I'll see him now. Just send him over this way."

Theo sprinted off just as an exhausted Fred Price dropped his legs to the ground.

"Let me repeat myself, Price," Warner threatened, "I do not have a problem moving Walden to left tackle and leaving you on the sideline."

Fred sat up and propped his arms on his knees. "I'm just slap give out Coach," he said in winded condition. "Give us a rest. We've been going non-stop all month, and there's another week to go, yet."

"And that's my dilemma, Price," the Coach pointed out, "how many flapjacks and mugs of cider will you consume by game time?"

Hodgson walked upon the scene and extended his right hand while retrieving his pad and pencil with his left.

"Good morning, Pop. I take it this is a good time for you?"

"As good as any, Harry. It seems my three *girls* here need a break anyhow."

Hodgson chuckled. The three players stood up.

"Don't drift off too far and report back on my whistle," Warner ordered. "Cow, tell all the other boys to take ten."

They wasted no time and headed off, but Warner kept one eyeball on them.

"Problem with those three?" Harry inquired.

"No problem, just a bit lethargic at times," Pop replied. "These two weeks between Sewanee and Auburn are tough. My stomach has been in knots." He made a fist and declared, "Gotta win this one, you know."

Harry was quick to agree, "Yes, beat Auburn and all the people of Georgia will celebrate our first undefeated season. Speaking for the class of ninety-three, we are all excited."

With a little hesitancy, Warner grinned and nodded.

"And Heisman," Harry added, "I hear he showed up at Brisbane to watch you play Carolina."

"Yeah, he was there," Pop confirmed. "But I'm not surprised in the least."

"I guess he wanted to see that awful, slanted field for himself since your game will be held there, too," Harry suggested. "I'd imagine that you're developing various offensive maneuvers. You know, depending on whether you are heading up or down the field?"

With a slightly puzzled look on his face, Pop responded, "Yes . . . you bet we are, Harry."

"And of course, I'm sure he wanted to see your new talent, Von Gammon."

Warner nodded but was still deliberating the previous question.

"Speaking of Gammon, is he around?" asked Harry. "I made the trip over from Atlanta today in part so I could ask him a few questions. I tried to speak with him after the Carolina game but ran into his over-protective mother who *denied access*."

"Yeah, I'm not sure if his mama cares for me much either, Harry. Or any football man for that matter."

"Well, I suppose this would be a good time to speak with him then, unless she is lurking in the bushes somewhere," Harry joked.

"That would be fine with me, Harry, but Von is not here," Pop revealed.

Harry shrugged his shoulders, and Warner hesitated before reporting the full story.

"It's his mother, you see," Pop began. "Since we play Auburn on Thanksgiving Day, she insisted that he come home today and spend a long weekend with the family."

"And you agreed to her terms?" Harry asked.

Pop took in a deep breath, "Yes, I did. She insisted that Von needed some quiet time away from all of this to catch up on studies and attend church with his family. He needs to 'stay grounded,' is how I think she put it, and quite frankly was rather convincing."

"Well, I can personally attest that she is quite skilled in getting what she wants," Hodgson said while taking pencil to paper.

"What are you writing, there?" Warner asked. "If it's all the same to you I'd prefer you keep these personal details off the record."

"The people want to know how the team is preparing for Auburn," Harry said as he scribbled out notes.

Pop placed his hand over Harry's right wrist to stop him from writing, "Von is only missing this one day of practice, and he promised to spend time riding his bicycle over the weekend to stay fit. And believe me, that boy never stops. I bet he'll get in more conditioning work than anyone else on this squad – he's probably getting in his daily calisthenics regimen on the train ride home."

"Seems you have developed quite a bit of trust with him," Harry asserted. "Allowing him to go home and condition on his own, for example."

"Why wouldn't I?"

"I don't know? Because he's only a freshman, perhaps?" Harry sarcastically suggested. "You're keeping a closer eye on your upperclassmen than him."

Warner was confident in his response, "Von doesn't act like a typical freshman. The way he led our team and competed against Sewanee; why, you would never guess that he is one if you didn't know it. I've never seen a youngster progress as quickly as he has."

"Sounds like you're ready to make him team captain," Harry commented.

"Nah," Warner scoffed. "Nalley is my captain. Gammon is just a freshman."

* * *

Von had taken the first-morning train out of Athens and arrived at the Rome station just before noon. Many at the depot recognized him, not only because he was back in his hometown, but because he was a star on the Red and Black football team. Most folks north of Macon had heard or read the name "Von Gammon" by now.

Monty was there to welcome him, which turned out to be a good thing. His tall frame and long arms helped maneuver Von through the crowd in a timely manner. Just about everyone they passed wanted to congratulate him or shake his hand, but Monty managed to keep them moving at a brisk pace.

At the house, Von was treated to a delicious home cooked meal with the family around the dining table. It was all smiles and laughter. Will had taken great interest in his now famous brother and made sure to sit next to him so he could hear everything Von had to say.

After lunch, Will begged his big brother to toss the football in the front yard, and Von obliged.

"Thanks for playing ball with me, Von," Will said after making a successful catch. "I don't understand why, but I'm guessing you would probably rather be smooching on Emily's face right now."

"It's alright," his brother returned, "she and I will have plenty of time for that this weekend. But promise to keep that between you and me, okay?"

"Yeah, no problem. I think it's gross anyway; swapping spit and all that," Will stated before changing the subject. "So, what's college life like? Anything interesting besides football?"

"Sure, we just finished reading a Mark Twain book about Joan of Arc in my literature class. I actually enjoyed it," Von attested.

Will stuck out his tongue before, "Yuck. I hate kissing *and* reading. I was hoping you were into something manlier than both of those things."

"I suppose playing football makes up the manly part," Von said, "but now that I'm at university, I've begun appreciating some of the premier literary works. But I still read thc sporting magazines, too."

Will didn't believe the story, at least the part about premier literary works. "Tell the truth, big brother; you're only reading those fancy books to impress Emily."

"I'm sorry to disappoint you, but Emily or no Emily I have discovered an appreciation for the classics."

This topic was of little interest to Will, so he tried to change it again.

"What else are you doing?"

Von thought for a moment before, "I've also learned a lot about recent industrial advancements, like the diesel engine and hydroelectric power."

"I don't understand any of that," Will grunted.

"You will soon enough. They say these things will change the world dramatically during the next century."

"Speaking of advances," Will interjected, "we're supposed to have a telephone in the house someday soon."

"Yes, and that's wonderful news! I saw all of the poles they've put up during my ride over from the train station," Von replied enthusiastically. "That means I'll be able to speak with y'all anytime, all the way from Athens. And Emily, too. How soon is soon?"

"You'll have to ask Father. All I know is they finished hanging all that wire a few weeks ago."

Will pointed up to the phone lines that ran down both sides of Third Avenue. However, Von noticed an oddity. Unlike the other houses, there was no line strung across the front of their lot. Instead, the wire coming up their side of the street crossed at both corners of their yard and ran parallel with the house along the other side of the road.

After a couple more tosses of the ball, Von asked Will to catch him up on current events at home, and Will had lots to say, "All Father has done for weeks is gripe about the vote for president because his man lost. He says the fella that won had a lot more money to spend on his campaign, and that he also wants to stop giving away free silver, or something like that. Pa's been real upset, and I guess I can't blame him. I mean, why would anybody turn down free silver?"

"Ah yes," Von said with a toss of the ball, "politics. Now that's something that *I* have little interest in. Maybe when we beat Auburn this Thursday, he'll forget about all of that and cheer up."

Will grinned and nodded before, "Hey, I saw Mother get all worked up when you first got home today. What did you say to her?"

"Oh, it was nothing," Von said as he held up his right arm and pointed to a bruise. "She noticed this whip on my arm. I got it on the gridiron."

"Oooh, that looks bad. Does it hurt?"

"Maybe a little when it happened, but not anymore. And seeing that I got it while making a first down helped ease the pain a little," Von remarked with a smirk.

They threw the ball a few more times before Von proclaimed, "It annoys me that she still worries about me so much. It's a real distraction."

"Well, I may be young, but I already know that mothers worry. She'll let me do pretty much everything I want, but she also has to know where I am going to be all the time. I have no privacy," Will protested.

Von chuckled, "You're too young to need privacy, Will." He paused before, "Do you ever worry about me, brother?"

"Not really and why would I? You're the toughest fella I know."

Von returned a smile. Just then, following another toss of the ball, Von held his right arm and winced in pain.

* * *

BRISBANE PARK, ATLANTA, GA
THANKSGIVING DAY; THURSDAY, NOVEMBER 26, 1896

The nearly three thousand spectators that attended the Georgia - North Carolina game had been considered a huge crowd. But on this day, that number was shattered.

It was estimated that more than eight thousand people filled the grounds at Brisbane for the Georgia - Auburn game that year. Most were able to get inside the park, but those less fortunate watched from wherever they could get a glimpse of the field. That included nearby roof and treetops for those spry enough to do so.

Tickets for the grandstand seats were so hard to get that Monty was limited to four. Nellie, J.A., and Rosalind joined him, and they packed together like a tin of sardines in the bleachers.

"I'm so glad that Emily was kind enough to invite Will over to her house to dine with her folks today," J.A. commented.

As she took in the surrounding sights and sounds, Rosalind replied, "Honestly, John, I don't know what this world is coming to. I mean, who would have ever predicted that this many people would prioritize a football game over spending time around the table with their family on Thanksgiving. It's truly unbelievable."

With a dash of sarcasm, Monty defended, "But Mother, we're family, and we're together. Most of us, anyway."

The fans clad in red and black outfits slightly outnumbered those wearing the orange and blue colors of Auburn, but both sides were well represented. There were so many bodies massed around the field that the two teams struggled to pass through them on the way to their respective sideline. But Thomas Reed found enough space to march about the field and wave his stick high in the air.

An enormous flood of cheers and applause rolled through the park as patrons clamored for their team of choice. Many of those cheers soon turned to jeers as supporters on both sides showered displeasure upon their hated rival, who was also before them.

One of the game officials trotted out to midfield to meet with the team captains from both schools. The first player to sprint out was Reynolds Tichenor of Auburn, a skinny lad that weighed less than 120 pounds, even when wearing football gear.

Cow Nalley slumbered out and arrived a minute or two after Tichenor. He was slightly taller and much thicker than Reynolds. They were quite the pair standing next to one another.

"Listen up, captains," the official announced, "as the home team, Georgia will call heads or tails while the coin is in the air. The winner of the toss will be awarded first possession and determine which side of the field you want to defend. Understood?"

"Yes, and thank you, kind sir," Tichenor politely replied.

A look from the official to Cow prompted a grunt in the affirmative.

Reynolds addressed Cow, and with a big smile and confident swagger said, "May the best team be victorious today, my large friend."

"I'm gonna step on your little head and flatten your face today, you little weasel," was the reply.

"All right then," Reynolds reacted, "looking forward to a rousing match today, big fella."

Nalley grunted again before turning his attention back toward the official, who tossed the coin into the air.

"Heads!" Cow yelled.

The silver dollar landed and rolled to a stop, revealing the face of Lady Liberty. The Red and Black had won the toss, and the Georgia crowd hollered with delight following the signal from the official.

Before making his decision, Nalley paused to survey both ends of the sloped field. A noticeable wind was blowing uphill.

"We'll defend the south goal and take the ball toward the north," he decided.

The official motioned Nalley's decision which was followed by more fan noise as they anxiously awaited play to begin.

Before parting for the sidelines, Reynolds offered, "I've enjoyed our short time out here together, chap. Best of luck to you."

"You'd best watch out for yourself, runt. Before this day is over, I'm gonna break that pretty little nose of yours with the heel of my shoe!" warned Nalley.

"War Eagle, then, big fellow!" Tichenor declared. He then turned and shivered off toward the sideline while Nalley remained in place, glaring him down from behind.

Kickoff came some five minutes later, with Hatton Lovejoy beginning the game with a significant return for Georgia. The first two carries by U of G backs led to little gain. It almost seemed as if the Auburn players had picked up on the Georgia play-calling signals before each scrimmage began, as they adjusted their formation in perfect defensive positions both times.

On third down, Von moved into punting position. After a good snap, he boomed a kick that soared over the receiving Auburn player's head. The punt was as impressive as it was unexpected, especially considering that he was punting uphill.

Neither team could do much on offense during the first half, and Auburn continued to do a brilliant job of anticipating the direction of Georgia's every rush play. However, Lovejoy managed to carry one across the goal line that provided a slim lead for the Red and Black at intermission.

Up in the stands, J.A. shouted, "Blazes, what a ball game! Halftime and our boys lead six to zero!"

"Thank you for the update, John," Rosalind replied. "I have been so entranced by that odd man prancing up and down the sideline that I'd lost track of the score."

"That there is Thomas Reed. He's most likely Georgia's most spirited fanatic."

"Fanatic?" Rosalind considered. "Well, I'd agree that is an appropriate description for him."

As intermission came to a close, both squads appeared from underneath the grandstands and ran out onto the field simultaneously. The two teams crossed paths on the way to their sidelines, allowing an opportunity for some smack-talk then pushing and shoving along the way. That little show primed the crowd for what was assuredly going to be a rousing second half.

The Red and Black lined up to kick off as the Tigers of Auburn prepared to receive. Before Von put the ball into play, he glanced over at Cow, who gave a quick wink of the eye – the trick play was on.

Gammon trotted toward the ball, but instead of kicking it far downfield as he'd done in the first half, he intentionally clipped the top of the ball with his foot, bouncing it a short distance down the left-hand side of the field. All of the Georgia men quickly ran ahead of the ball and created a human shield in front of Cow, allowing him to jump on top of the loose ball before Auburn had an opportunity to pick it up.

The referee awarded possession to U of G, which led to a huge celebration by all those wearing red. Elated, the Georgia team jumped up and down while the befuddled Tigers argued with the officials over the call. Alas, Coach Heisman ran out onto the field and ordered that his boys take defensive positions before the Red and Black could run a play.

"An unbelievable turn of events!" Monty cheered from his seat.

"Yes, a brilliant play indeed!" chimed J.A. "As long as that sort of thing is even legal by the rulebook, that is."

"And that Reed fellow is certainly happy," Rosalind noted.

Once the head official confirmed that the ball belonged to Georgia, both teams lined up for the next play from scrimmage. Von was joined in the backfield by Nalley, Lovejoy, and another back named Laurie Cothran.

To stymie the Tiger defense, there was no verbal signal called by Georgia before this play. After a silent snap, Von faked a hand-off to Cow and Hatton, only to reverse his tread and flip the ball to Cothran, who was running in the opposite direction and away from all of the blockers.

Not fooled by the play, one lone defender stayed his position and was ready to take down the Georgia ball carrier. However, Von saw this and made a beeline toward the Tiger. From out of nowhere,

Gammon hammered the Auburn player and sent him to the ground, allowing Cothran to run untouched all the way and across the goal line.

The grandstands shook and swayed with frenzied celebration. Assuredly, no baseball game had ever put this much pressure on the timbers that supported the thousands of souls who had come out to root for their team.

From opposing sidelines, the two coaches locked in a stare. Heisman dropped his hands on his hips, tucked his lip, and nodded to Warner. He'd been outsmarted by the man from Cornell.

The successful conversion kick from Gammon that followed triggered another grimace from Heisman. The score was 12-0 with all of the momentum on the side of Georgia.

# HALFTIME

*As you recall, Von and the boys went on to defeat Auburn that Thanksgiving Day in 1896, although Reynolds Tichenor nearly tied the game on a late punt return. It's a good thing Cow Nalley got in his way just shy of the goal line.*

*I remember the newspaper headlines praising Warner for beating Heisman and going undefeated for the season. But I suppose the bigger headline came months later when Pop announced that he was leaving Athens to coach ball at Cornell University, his alma mater. Von was enamored with Pop and stressed over the news.*

*I think it was Walter who convinced him to finally pledge the SAE fraternity over the winter, which they did together. After that, his school work improved, and he eventually seemed less worried about Pop's departure.*

*Baseball season came with the warming of spring, and Von played third base exceptionally well. Ironically, his rival Tichenor transferred to Georgia to attend law school and ended up covering second base in the same infield. They were teammates on paper, but I get the sense that was about the extent of their relationship.*

*He came home that summer and spent his mornings helping out at the store before spending the afternoons with Emily. Monty and*

*Nellie had their first baby in June, and our newly extended family went to Church together on Sundays and ate many a meal around that big table that you loved so much.*

*Toward the end of August, I found myself becoming terrifically excited for the approaching football season. That's when Von gave us a little scare; hurting his leg like he did while preparing for that big bicycle race in Atlanta. He was looking forward to competing in that event and was quite downtrodden for a spell afterward.*

*Even still, I assumed the anticipation of football season would lift his spirits, but he struggled with that injury longer than expected. If you recall, he arrived in Athens a couple of weeks late before his sophomore year. Perhaps that delay had more to do with the angst of leaving Emily behind in Rome for another year instead of simply waiting for his leg to heal.*

*It's easy to look back and see it now, but little did we know then that the leaves of fall had marked an end to the happiest days of our lives.*

# SOPHOMORE JINX

OLD COLLEGE, UNIVERSITY OF GEORGIA CAMPUS
THURSDAY, SEPTEMBER 30, 1897

Von, J. A., Emily, and Will entered room 207 of the Old College Building, and the men set down suitcases of various sizes on what would once again be Von's bed during the upcoming school year. Walter's things were already in place.

"Well, it turned out to be a farce!" Will exclaimed. "For it was Mark Twain himself who was quoted as saying, 'The report of my death was an exaggeration'!"

The punch line had them all laughing.

J.A. looked at Von, "Can you believe what affection your young brother has suddenly taken toward reading?"

Von winked at Will before saying, "That's good to hear, little brother. Keep it up."

A nod from Will proceeded, "Hey, you can all stay here while I go and fetch the last bag."

"Alright, but don't stray," J.A. insisted. "Heaven forbid I lose you on this campus. Your mother would never forgive me."

"I'll go along with him," Emily offered. "Besides, I'd like to take in more of the campus scenery while I have the chance."

"Thank you, Emily," J.A. replied, "you're a real sweetheart."

Emily nodded and smiled, only to realize that Will had already left the room. In a beat, she was down the hall chasing after him.

Upon her exit, Von shared with J.A., "Her father's decision to keep her home and out of college here in Athens has left Emily heartbroken. Myself as well if I must be honest."

"I'd imagine it was a decision of necessity," J.A. comforted. "It's been a struggle for some folks to put food on the table these past several years. We've been quite fortunate."

"I can tell she's upset that we'll be separated from one another for a whole 'nother school year," Von confided.

J.A. tried to lighten the mood, "Just remember, 'tis absence that makes the heart grow fonder. You should know that phrase. It's from poetry."

"Yeah, I've heard it. Mother gave me that line once before. You two are on the ball with that one." There was something else that Von was eager to disclose, so he blurted it out, "I've decided to ask Emily for her hand in marriage."

Surprised by the remark, J.A. took a few steps back and contested, "What? I agree that Emily is a wonderful girl, but you've got three more years of school ahead of you. Does Monty and Nellie having a baby have anything to do with this rushed decision?"

"I'm happy for them, but no," Von declared. "I do want a family someday, but marriage will come after school is over. It's just that if I don't commit to her now, she might be won over by some other boy back home and I will lose her. I can't take that risk."

J.A. advised, "Marriage, or even a proposal, is a lifetime commitment and a very serious decision. I'd like you to take more time to consider this before you make a move. But if you choose to propose, ask for her father's blessing prior. And perhaps more important, discuss the matter with your mother."

Von returned the suggestion with a smirk and grumbled, "This year is going to turn out so much different than I had planned."

"I'm sure that McCarthy will be a fine coach," J.A. assured. "He is a Brown University man, so he must be a scholar. And from what I hear has a learned football mind."

"I just don't understand why Pop left us in such a hurry," Von explained. "We were becoming that great team he dreamed about. That I dreamed about."

"You're still a great team. And now that Cow is an assistant trainer, he will tell the new coach all about you and the others," J.A. suggested.

"I'm not so sure about that," Von replied.

J.A. shrugged his shoulders, leading Von to elaborate, "I don't think Cow ever took much of a liking to me. From day one he's held it against me that Pop started me as a freshman. Especially at quarterback."

"Then I suggest you try and befriend him immediately," J.A. recommended. "Cow is a university icon."

"I agree, and he knows that more than anyone, which is part of the problem. I'm sure he thinks staying on as a trainer will help maintain his *iconic* status."

A knock from behind interrupted the conversation, and they turned to see Cow standing in the dorm room, half-way through the open door. Von was red-faced and swallowed deep.

"So, it sounds like 'ya got the news," Cow said with a hint of hostility. "Don't 'cha think *Coach* Nalley sounds better than *Cow* Nalley?" he added with a snort.

Von stepped forward and extended a hand, but Cow chose to forego the shake and instead slapped him on the back. Hard.

"Believe me, Gammon, I begged Coach McCarthy to put me on the playing roster, but he said that all these wrinkles around my eyes would give my age away to the opposition," Cow said while pointing to his face. "So, I did the next best thing and accepted the coaching role."

Attempting some damage control, Von replied, "Wrinkles or not; it's no question that you'd still be one of the best on any football field, *Coach*."

Cow grunted back at Von but directed his next comment to his father, "And it's a pleasure to see you again, Mr. Gammon."

"Likewise, and congratulations on your coaching assignment."

Cow nodded in appreciation before J.A. added, "We were commenting on how fortunate Coach McCarthy is to have you on staff. We're all hoping for another undefeated season!"

That remark prompted Nalley to alert Von, "Speaking of Coach McCarthy, he's on the field with all the other boys. If you find the time this afternoon, trot over and say hello. I know he's been lookin' forward to meetin' 'ya. You're gonna see a few new faces on the squad, too."

"You bet. Once I get all my things put away, I will be there. I'm anxious to catch up and get started."

"You know," Nalley started, "there was some talk goin' around that you might not show this year, bein' so late to campus and all. But I kept tellin' Coach to hold a space for you."

Von was genuinely apologetic, "And I appreciate your support. I never expected to be sidelined like I was following my bike incident."

"And you're sure that you're ready to play?" Cow questioned. "We've got our first game with Clemson in just over a week, and nobody's been able to watch you run, yet."

Von responded emphatically, "I am absolutely, one-hundred percent ready to go, and at full speed no less. I just wanted to stay home a little while longer for some extra conditioning before I came back for another season on the gridiron."

The new coach seemed satisfied with the confident response, "Well, I for one am glad you showed up and look forward to introducin' 'ya to McCarthy here in a bit."

This time, Cow accepted Von's firm handshake.

"But until then, I've got someone else you should talk to."

"Who's that?" Von asked curiously.

Cow turned toward the dorm room door, "Come on in, Tick!"

Reynolds Tichenor entered from the hallway. He was wearing a black pullover with a red 'G' on the chest along with a hesitant smile on his face.

"Afternoon, Gammons," Tichenor chimed to both before approaching Von. "And greetings to you, my friend. It's been a while since we last saw each other out on the diamond."

Von's eyes were fixated on Reynold's sweater and did not speak.

Realizing that he was in a stupor, Tichenor reached out and tapped Von on the arm, "Since we rarely spoke to one another in the spring, I didn't get the chance to congratulate you on a well-played baseball season. You were spectacular on defense and a maestro with that bat of yours."

Not a peep from Von. He remained locked on the sweater.

Hoping to lighten the mood, Tichenor confessed with a chortle, "You know, Coach Nalley here frightened me so bad during our football game last year that I hesitated before transferring to Athens. But then I figured it was best to have a brute like him on my side and not the other," he said, snickering.

Von finally looked up from Reynold's chest, "No disrespect, Reynolds, but that vest just doesn't look right on you."

Tichenor looked down and stretched his shirt tight before responding, "On the contrary, Gammon, I've become quite fond of it. Perhaps you'd be happy to know that I've demoted my Auburn vest to nothing more than a seat cushion at this point."

Unimpressed, Von shrugged with indifference.

"Come on, Gammon," Tichenor pled, "you saw me play vigorously for this school out on the baseball field. Quite frankly, my change of loyalty is old news to most folks around town."

Von snapped back, "And I suppose you're here to tell me that you tried out for the football team, too?"

Reynolds peeked over at Cow, who nodded back with the 'go ahead' signal.

"Actually, yes. I attended tryouts like everyone else. That is, except you, of course," he added with a sarcastic grin. "No offense, friend. I know you've been hurt and I'm only joshing you."

Von shook his head and remained silent, so Tichenor continued, "I've already been assured a position on the team, so Coach Nalley thought it best that you and I speak now, in case there was any conflict we needed to address before we take the field together."

"No conflict, I suppose," Von professed, "as long as you give it your all as a Georgia man." He chuckled before admitting, "In fact, I'm a bit flattered that we've managed to convert a member of the enemy over to our side."

Cow spoke bluntly, "Reynolds is a quarterback by trade, so we're expecting he'll play the position this year instead of you."

The startling announcement silenced the room. J.A. turned quickly and peered at Von to gauge his reaction, but there was none. He simply stood and stared awkwardly at Reynolds.

"That's the conflict," Cow finished.

Von shook his head and questioned, "How could you make that decision before I even get here, Cow? I swear to you that I'm fully healed, and now that I'm back it seems logical that we should both try out for the position and let Coach McCarthy make the final choice."

This time, it was Cow who remained silent.

"I want to see Coach McCarthy," Von stated. "I'd like to see him *now*."

J.A. placed his hand on Von's shoulder to calm him, but his son moved out from under his grasp.

That's when Reynolds interjected, "Tell you what gentlemen, I've already over-extended my break and am due back on the field. Please excuse me from our chat." He nodded toward J.A., "It was a pleasure to meet you, Mr. Gammon. And Von, I'm sure that I'll see you on the field shortly."

With that, Reynolds darted out of the room.

"Come on, Cow . . . I mean, Coach Nalley. Why would you even *consider* Tichenor at quarterback?" Von implored. "Freshman or not, didn't I prove myself during our undefeated season? Heck, we even beat the team that he played quarterback for! Do I need to prove to everyone that my leg has healed, or is this something personal between you and me?"

"Nothing personal. Tick has four seasons at the position. You have one. I always choose experience."

Von disclosed, "I've had a bad feeling in my stomach ever since I heard that Coach Warner was leaving."

"Just get out there and show the fellas what you can do," J.A. advised. "That's how you got the quarterback position last year. Do it again."

Cow informed, "Don't forget, Von, that you also kick and play hard defense. And since you're heavier than Tick, we'll use your strong legs at fullback. That is, as long as that one leg is as good as you say it is."

Von returned a sharp look of displeasure.

"As a man who claims to bleed red and black, how can you be upset that we've added someone to the lineup who can make our squad even better than last year?" Cow challenged.

Von proclaimed, "We were a great team last year, as is, and on our way to being even better this season."

Cow shrugged off the comment, leading Von to accuse, "You know what I think? I think you never liked that Pop started me at quarterback my first year, and this is your way to *make things right*. Am I right, *Coach* Cow?"

"You got some mouth on you, boy." Cow returned. "I am the Assistant Trainer, and you'd dang better show me some respect if you want my help getting any playin' time at all. Lovejoy ain't around no more to take up for you."

Von glared at Cow and accused, "I know it was you that threw that brick through my window."

In an attempt to diffuse the building tension, J.A. stepped in between them, "Son, Cow is right. Shut your trap and prove yourself on the field."

"I've already done that, Father. Maybe Cow's bigger fear is that someone replaces him at the top of the U of G icon list. Someone like me, perhaps."

In a bold move, Cow pushed the elder Gammon out of the way and immobilized Von in a headlock with a fist held high in the air, ready to punch, "You little snot!"

Von struggled to get free, but Cow had already gained leverage and was able to keep him in his stronghold. Off balance, they fell as one into Walter's desk and crashed to the floor. Books and two broken chair legs scattered about the room.

J.A. tried to separate them, but Cow threatened, "Back off, old man! Unless you want me to beat two generations of Gammons at the same time!"

J.A. complied, and Nalley was able to maintain his lock on Von while scooting to a seated position up against the wall.

Von squirmed and fought but to no avail. J.A. just watched.

"Listen to your daddy and save your anger for the field," Cow huffed.

Just then, Will and Emily entered the room carrying that last bag. Their smiles and giggles ceased immediately upon seeing Von and Cow on the floor.

Emily put her hands on her cheeks and yelped, "Oh my God!"

At this, Cow released his captive and they both stood up quickly. Von had a bloody lip, and Emily ran to embrace him and then applied a hanky to his wound. After Von insisted that he was okay, she turned to Nalley, "What is wrong with you, you brute?!"

The room remained silent while Emily repeatedly inspected Von's injury. The men's eyes darted back and forth at one another, each anticipating the other's next move.

Cow finally made a concession, "My apologies, Miss," he directed toward Emily. "Your sweetie and I had a few things to work out, that's all."

J.A. frowned with disapproval at the Coach, and with that Cow turned to exit the room. At the door, he looked back at Von.

"I'll see you on the field, Gammon."

* * *

ALUMNI ATHLETIC FIELD, UNIVERSITY OF GEORGIA
THURSDAY, OCTOBER 7, 1897

The smell of fresh paint and the sounds of hammering permeated the air as workers completed final touches on new bleachers around the football field. Young blades of green grass were now plentiful atop what was once a barren, dirt surface. These upgrades were a reward of sorts that followed an undefeated season for the Red and Black.

But changes to the football program weren't limited to the field. Coach Charles, or 'Chas,' McCarthy was the new face on campus after being hired to replace Pop Warner. Chas, 24 and from Irish descent, had attended Brown University and graduated only one year prior. While there, he played on the football team and earned All-American honors. Some considered him rather short and thin to have possibly been a celebrated football player, but hidden underneath his clothing were well-toned muscles and broad shoulders.

Since school, he'd spent most of his time on what turned out to be a failed personal campaign to fight for the United States during the Spanish-American War. When he first tried to enlist, the military denied his application due to certain physical limitations. Undeterred, Chas traveled to Florida, where he was discovered trying to sneak aboard a ship full of soldiers and cast back ashore.

Before the fall of '97, McCarthy accepted the coaching position at Georgia and used the salary to pay for a spot in law school. His life was back on track and he was proud to inspect the new facility alongside Dr. Charles Herty, a.k.a. "The Father of Georgia Football."

Herty was 30; six years McCarthy's elder. His salt and pepper colored hair and round spectacles topped off an intelligent look about him.

But the intelligent part didn't stop with mere appearance. Herty was a Georgia native who had elected to go north and earn a doctorate from Johns Hopkins University in Baltimore. During his time there, Herty learned about and came to love the game of football, and afterward brought his new-found passion down south when he returned to Athens in 1891 to become an instructor of chemistry.

Although he became an esteemed chemist later in life, Athenians knew him at the time as the man who revitalized the athletic programs at the University. And most importantly – founded the football program.

His first project upon arrival was to start a varsity baseball team, on which he played center-field. Soon after, he organized the school's very first football club, with Cow Nalley being one of its founding members. In January of 1892, that team played its inaugural game at home on the dirt; a 50-0 win over Mercer University of Macon, Georgia. The final tally was likely more lop-sided than that. It was reported that the official scorer temporarily left the game in its late hour to purchase booze at a distillery across the street. In doing so, he missed at least one U of G touchdown.

The following month, Herty squared off against one of his college pals from John Hopkins, George Petrie, who as a history professor had started a football team of his own at Auburn. Thus, began the 'Deep South's Oldest Rivalry,' as the series is known today.

Georgia vs. Auburn 1892 was played at Piedmont Park in Atlanta. The newspapers proclaimed that "Atlanta was wild over the matter," and pundits estimated that somewhere between two and three thousand spectators paid $0.50 for an adult ticket or $0.25 for a child to see what the fledgling sport was all about.

The Red and Black were accompanied onto the field that day by their first mascot – a goat named Sir William that was draped in black fabric with the letters 'U.G.' stitched in red. Despite great enthusiasm, Herty's squad came up short and lost 0-10 following a rain-soaked second-half.

But there was a strong feeling of optimism heading into the 1897 season, as the win from the '96 Georgia squad had tied the overall series record with Auburn at two games each. Even better, it was the victory that capped off an undefeated record. And that's what led to the construction of new bleachers, the planting of real grass, and the hiring of an All-American.

"Welcome to the new Alumni Athletic Field, Chas," Herty said proudly to McCarthy as they walked upon the scene. "We somehow managed to rise to the top using some of the poorest equipment in the South, including our old red dirt field. But the alumni were so enthused over last season that they organized an effort to raise enough funds for all of the improvements seen before you," he said with outstretched arms.

"And their enthusiasm comes with good reason, Dr. Herty," the young coach commended. "However, I'd like to remind you that we'll line up against some tough competition this fall. Perhaps my predecessor got an early glimpse of the schedule before making his decision to leave?"

They chuckled over that remark.

"But seriously," McCarthy continued, "I will ensure success remains constant here in Athens, no matter the opponent."

Pausing their stride, Herty lowered his specs and looked straight into the new coach's eyes, "We hired you for a reason, Chas. Regardless of recent success, it feels like a good time for change. With a new trainer and a new playing field, I intend to turn the Georgia football program into what I envision as the 'Yale of the South'."

"The passion for excellence is evident and appreciated," Chas responded, "and I am impressed with how the boosters raised the amount of money required to make these upgrades."

The two began their stroll again with Herty saying, "I should note that a good portion of the nineteen-hundred dollars raised came from the Butterfly Fete, which is staged by the *women* in our community."

"If I may, sir, recommend to the alumni group that someday they name this field after you. For if there had been no Charles Herty at Georgia, there would have been no football, either."

Herty snickered and replied, "That's mighty fine of you to say, Chas, but you realize the job is already yours!"

After a shared laugh and friendly handshake, Herty asked McCarthy about his initial impression of the team.

"Well, we lost Hatton Lovejoy to graduation, and I understand that he was a strong runner out of the backfield and a mighty fine player all around. But the good news is that most of the other lads from last year's team are back," he informed. "There's a fellow named J.T. Moore who has shown solid potential at the halfback position."

"Do you think he will grind out enough yards to equal that of Lovejoy?"

"Probably not on his own," the coach conceded, "but with Gammon now at fullback we'll have lots of options rushing the ball."

Herty stopped in his tracks, "Gammon? At fullback?"

"Yes, sir, that's correct," McCarthy said confidently. "The Auburn transfer – uh, Tichenor – he'll run the offense at quarterback this year."

The announcement on its merit did not satisfy Herty's curiosity or reservation over the change, so McCarthy detailed more reasons why he'd selected Tichenor to replace Gammon behind center.

"Very well. You are our head man, and therefore I respect the decision," Herty granted as they resumed their walk, "but Gammon is very athletic and strong."

"Tichenor is quick on his feet, and don't be fooled by his petite stature," McCarthy cautioned. "Despite his size, I've witnessed a mature leader who is quite vocal and constantly encourages the other men. He's also very intelligent and makes good decisions with the football."

The two arrived upon members of the squad who had gathered on the opposite end of the field to greet Dr. Herty and Coach McCarthy.

Von and Reynolds flanked each side of the group with Cow Nalley standing in the rear. Price and Walden were a couple more familiar faces from the '96 team that were back for another season.

McCarthy bellowed, "Most of you fellows, if not all of you, know Dr. Herty. He is the Physical Director here at the University."

The players nodded, and some offered polite verbal greetings.

"We are grateful to now have such an exquisite field to play upon," McCarthy expressed. "Clemson comes calling this Saturday, and it is important that we christen our new turf with a victory!"

The team cheered as Chas continued, "And, in Dr. Herty's presence, I would like to announce that Billy Kent will be our team captain this season!"

Kent raised his arms and was congratulated with many cheers, slaps on the back, and rubs of the head.

McCarthy hushed the crowd and informed them that he'd posted the starting roster for Saturday's game outside the door of the basement dressing room.

Team Captain Kent hollered out, "So Coach . . . whose gonna play quarterback? Von or Tick?"

The question aroused the others, and they clamored for an answer.

"Alright," McCarthy calmed, "I know that's one that you've all been wondering about. Particularly, Gammon and Tichenor, I'd imagine."

The group nodded and cried out again, leading McCarthy to cut to the chase.

"Gammon," he said with a glance toward Von, "you will start at fullback." He looked toward Reynolds and confirmed, "And Tick, you will take snaps from center."

What followed was an emotionally mixed reaction from members of the team, and they all stared at Von to catch his response. But there was no dramatic reaction. All that came was a respectful nod from Von that acknowledged the coach's final verdict.

"Everyone else, check the roster for your position," McCarthy directed. "Use tomorrow to rest your bones and be here early on Saturday, ready for battle!"

The team dispersed in different directions, including Von who walked away alone.

Assessing Von's dour mood, Reynolds grabbed a football and jogged up behind him.

"Hey, Von! Wait up!"

Von halted and reversed course to face Tichenor, "I'm sorry, Reynolds. Guess I forgot to congratulate you." Without emotion, Von uttered, "Congratulations."

After that, Von turned his back on Tichenor and continued walking away.

"Hold on, chap. Let's discuss the matter."

Von picked up his pace, and while still looking ahead assured, "There's nothing to discuss. Coach made his decision, and that's that." He then suddenly stopped and spun around as a thought entered his mind, "Besides, it's the only position you can play. I can play others; fullback, kicker, and linebacker to name a few. So, it's no big deal."

Again, Von headed off in the opposing direction, but Reynolds sped past him to intercept.

"No, this *is* a big deal," Tichenor proclaimed as Von took in a deep, defensive breath. "Look, I understand my joining the club came as an unpleasant surprise to you. And to be honest, when I enrolled in law school, I had no intentions of playing football."

"So why *are* you playing then?"

Reynolds let out a sigh of his own and confessed, "Because Coach Nalley asked that I consider it. I suppose being courted by someone got me excited about the idea."

"I don't need to be wooed by anyone. I am always excited for football," Von declared. "And in my opinion, Cow recruiting you is all a part of some personal vendetta that he's had against me since the day I first stepped on that old dirt field."

Von tried to maneuver around Reynolds, but his arm was taken, holding him in place.

"Come on, Gammon," Tick pleaded. "Stop thinking of me as the enemy. You and I will make a great tandem out there."

"And what of the day we play Auburn?" Von charged. "Coach Warner instilled it in us to despise them. To me, you're just an Auburn fellow disguised in a Georgia jacket. Heck, how do I know that you're not here to spy for Coach Heisman? I know he's tricky like that."

Reynolds shook his head in disbelief while Von made another accusation, "Everybody knows you're from the same cloth; maybe worse."

"Yeah? How so?"

"Look no further than the '95 Vandy game when you hid the ball under your jersey to cheat a touchdown," Von accused. "It's only fitting that your team still lost that game."

"There were no rules against that trick," Tichenor defended. "Instead of cheating, I'd call it innovation."

Without a word, Von pulled his arm free from his captive and began walking away, but Reynolds kept up with him step for step.

"Listen, I know you've put a lot of heart into this team, but let me give you some advice; part of growing up is accepting change and adapting to circumstances, like it or not," Tick argued.

Again, he managed to move in front of Von, bringing him to a standstill.

"Take the ball and run with it," Reynolds offered while extending the ball toward him.

Von glimpsed down at the football but chose not to take it, saying "Don't worry about me. I will give my all for this team and show no ill toward you in front of others."

"I sure hope you get over yourself, Gammon. Remember that after it's all said and done, football is nothing more than a game."

Reynolds shoved the ball into Von's chest, at which point he did take it.

"I will lay it all out on the field against our opponents, including Auburn," Tick vowed. "But I can also *leave* it on the field when the game is over."

After an abrupt turnabout, Tichenor trotted off, leaving Von standing alone with the ball.

* * *

SHUTE'S BARBER SHOP, ROME, GA
SATURDAY, OCTOBER 9, 1897

For years, Alan Shute's place on Broad Street had been a favorite gathering spot for the men of Rome, and not just for a shave and cut.

Like in many small towns across America, Shute's had become a place for fellas to socialize, hold meetings, or get away from home, work, or their wives for an hour or two.

By the fall of '97, a relatively new activity had become popular on Saturdays during the months of October and November. With the assistance of a telegrapher named Gaylord Jones, Shute's offered a space where upwards of twenty men could pile into the modest size shop, huddle around Mr. Jones, and listen to him announce the on-field action of a college football game, almost in real time via the telegraph.

Naturally, the two most common teams 'broadcast live' were the University of Georgia and the Georgia School of Technology, but ever since the local Gammon kid had become a star in Athens, it was Red and Black games that drew the largest crowds. That also meant that Georgia contests received priority status should the two schools play on the same day.

Two ornate barber chairs anchored a full-length wall mirror. Each was carved from oak and upholstered with fine leather. Simpler chairs were pushed up against the perimeter walls with the telegrapher seated at a table in the middle of it all. Although not required for admission, it was expected that at some point during the afternoon, each man would take a turn in one of the big chairs with either Alan or his side-kick Ben for some grooming action.

The all-male U of G partisan crowd that had filed in for the clash versus Clemson was delighted to discover Von's father and brother in attendance. The barbers were quick to serve J.A. and Monty – on the house – and they were the center of everyone's attention for most of the first half. No matter, Gaylord went diligently about his business and announced the result of every play, regardless of whether anyone was listening or not. Eventually, the novelty of having real-live Gammons in their presence waned, and everyone settled in for the remainder of the broadcast.

Jones read aloud, "Result of the play is a twelve-yard gain for Georgia and a first down on the Clemson eight-yard line."

That resulted in a jubilant cry from the patrons.

"I feel another score coming if they'll run my boy around the end again," J.A. exclaimed. His statement was quickly seconded by almost every man in the place.

Monty leaned over toward his father to speak in confidence, "It's nice to spend the day here with you, Father. You know I love my Nellie and the baby, but a man needs to get away from time to time for some well-intended male bonding."

J.A. flashed a smile and chirped, "I agree. It's darn good for the soul, isn't it, son? Especially when we're bonding over football!"

Monty agreed.

"And it's good that our wives understand this need of ours and allow us to enjoy a wholesome ball game with all these fine fellows around," J.A. added.

"So, Mother knows where you are then, correct?" Monty asked.

J.A. cracked an expression of disappointment, "Of course she does, son. I'll admit that when I told her about our plans, I sensed she'd liked to have joined us; if she could, that is. But she's occupied with washing the linens, and this deal here is a man-only thing, anyway," he finished with a smirk.

"Ball dropped by Tichenor," announced Gaylord.

The room groaned.

He followed with, "Recovered by Waldren of Georgia."

The room simultaneously sighed with relief.

"Second down for Georgia, now on the eleven-yard line."

"What did I say before? Give the ball to Gammon!" J.A. hollered. Many of the men clapped and cheered in support.

"I must admit," Monty confessed, "I feel a tad guilty being here while Nellie is burdened with the baby at home alone. Do you feel the least bit guilty about leaving Mother with those chores while we're out reveling?"

J.A. snapped his neck toward Monty, this time sporting a look of confusion, "Guilty? Blazes, no, Monty! Your mother loves to labor over the wash. I mean, if she didn't why in Heaven's name would she take all blasted day to do it?"

Gaylord reported, "Tichenor keeps the ball and tackled at the nine-yard line."

"That's a lousy two yards!" a man cried with a slap of his knee. "You are right, J.A.! Why doesn't Coach just give the ball to your boy?"

Others gripe over the matter.

J.A. smiled and waved at the man who spoke out before continuing his conversation with Monty, "And besides, we're not just out fooling around. We both got a shave and a haircut. That's a productive use of our time if you ask me."

"Good point, Father," Monty credited. "And it was a free cut at that!"

"All the better," J.A. resolved. "Speaking of Nellie and the baby, have I mentioned that Von is planning on asking Emily to marry him?"

"Marriage? Why, he's just a baby himself!"

Gaylord belted, "Gammon runs around the end for a U of G touchdown!"

The whole place erupted in celebration. Several men came over to J.A. and Monty to shake hands and pat them on the back. Just as things calmed down a bit, the telegrapher informed everyone that Von's conversion kick was successful, making the score 18-0 in favor of the Red and Black. That led to more handshaking and slapping for the next few minutes.

Once free from the glad-handing, Monty got back on point, "Von is getting married, and you approved? Just like that?"

"No, not now. After college. He just wants to secure Emily's hand, like a promissory note. I'm not sure when he plans to propose, but I told him to be sure and get her father's blessing first."

"I suppose that part won't be very easy," Monty suggested. "You can't do that sort of thing over the telegraph."

At that moment, the bells on the front door chimed, and all eyes were on Rosalind as she stepped inside the shop.

"Mother!" Monty proclaimed. "What a pleasant surprise!"

"Well hello, love," J.A. mustered.

Rosalind snipped at J.A., "I was out back hanging all the whites when I realized you hadn't returned home yet, so I wanted to come down here and see what a two-hour haircut was all about."

Monty glared at his father and shrugged his shoulders.

"Kickoff received by Clemson. Returned to own thirty-three yard-line," Gaylord decreed with one eye on his equipment and the other on Rosalind.

Alan left his customer and ambled over to welcome her, "Good afternoon, Mrs. Gammon. Nice to see you again. Your son is playing one heckuva ball game today. Why, he just scored a touchdown!"

"Thank you, Mr. Shute," she returned. "It's nice of you to provide the fellows a place to gather." With a glance toward J.A., she asked, "You want to tell me why I don't know anything about this?"

Monty interjected, "For the record, Nellie knows exactly where I am and exactly what we are doing, Mother. In fact, with the game in hand, I believe that I'll return to her now."

He kissed his mother on the cheek before turning to J.A., "Have a good afternoon, Father." With that, the ringing of bells sounded his exit.

Gaylord read out another game update, but the majority of onlookers were more interested in the family drama unfolding in front of them.

"Listen, Rosie," J.A. pled, "I know I didn't mention anything about staying here after getting our trim, but when I discovered these gents were listening to a live account of the game, why, I couldn't resist."

Rosalind gave a sharp look back, "I'm not upset about the football, John. But I don't like the deceit."

"You have every right to be upset with me, dear. And although I am where I told you I'd be, I understand why you would interpret . ."

"Tell you what," she interrupted with a finger placed upon J.A.'s lips, "since I'm here now why don't I take Monty's place and listen to my boy play some football?"

A little stunned, J.A. nodded and prepared the empty chair before Rosalind took a seat.

Suddenly, "Clemson fumble, recovered by Gammon on the Georgia twenty-five!"

Rosalind was back on her feet in an instant, cheering along with all the men.

# THE COMPETITION

*By the time we made the trek to Athens for the match-up with Georgia Tech, I think you'd realized that playing football at the University was the most cherished thing in Von's young life. Other than Emily, of course. You also knew that on the inside, he was heartbroken over losing the quarterback position to Reynolds, but he wouldn't dare let anyone see that on the outside. No matter the obstacles, he was still the brightest star on the team.*

*At least he was to you and me.*

ATHENS, GA
SATURDAY, OCTOBER 23, 1897

The majority of passengers that shared an open train cabin with the Gammons were dressed in their red and black attire and repeatedly recited victory chants along the way, such as:

*Georgia, Georgia*
*Rah, Rah!*
*Hoo, Rah! Hoo, Rah!*
*Varsity! Varsity!*
*Rah! Rah! Rah!!*

J.A. and Rosalind did their best to participate in the miniature pep-rally, but there were times when they stopped yelling just to catch their breath. There were a handful of travelers onboard who had no interest in the outcome of the day's upcoming football contest, but they were easygoing and no one complained. If nothing else, it was an entertaining atmosphere.

The rail car pulled into the downtown Athens station only twenty minutes before the scheduled kick-off, requiring the Georgia faithful to rush down the sidewalks and past 'The Gate' to make it to the Athletic Field in time.

Squads from U of G and Georgia Tech had only faced each other one prior time, back in 1893. But that 'game' turned into something perhaps better described as an 'incident' and created a rivalry that instilled so much disdain for one another that a rematch had been put off for four years.

The initial point of contention stemming from that first match came from the Georgia side. Tech had supplemented its roster with non-traditional students, including a 33-year-old Army surgeon and talented ball player by the name of Leonard Wood. Additionally, one of the two referees assigned to the game turned out to be the brother of the Tech trainer. During the contest, Georgia people began chanting:

*Well, well, well*
*Who can tell?*
*The Tech's umpire cheats like hell!*

Georgia fanatics became so irate that during the second half they showered their opponent with dirt clods and rocks, one of which struck Wood in the face and opened a cut above the eye. But that didn't stop the sturdy surgeon as he rambled in for a touchdown even after suffering the bloody injury. The visitors from Tech handily beat the home team by a score of 28-6.

After the final whistle, the Georgia faithful capped off an ugly day by pelting the 'Techies' with more rocks and dirt as they headed back to their train. Thus, began the series that is now called 'Clean Old-Fashioned Hate.'

Tech's fight song was composed that same night during a very difficult train ride back to Atlanta. At the close of the tune, they added the now famous post-script, "To Hell With Georgia!" That trip in itself is a whole 'nother story.

Perhaps fortunate for all involved, the Red and Black took control of the '97 game early and cruised to a 28-0 shutout win without any significant uprising between the two teams.

Von played a stellar game on both sides of the ball. Each time he rushed for a first down, he made a point to find his mother in the crowd, kiss the football, and hold it out in her direction. She returned each tribute by blowing a kiss back to her son.

At the end of the game, J.A. and Rosalind sought Von out and embraced him after such a fine performance. This was the first time they'd seen him play on his home turf, and the outpouring of admiration toward Von from all of the U of G folks seemed almost overwhelming. They'd been chomping at the bit for a win like this over Tech, and Von had helped them do so.

Harry Hodgson from the paper walked straight past all the other players in his continued quest to land a one-on-one interview with

Von Gammon. This time, Rosalind did not interfere. She decided that it was time he speak to the world.

Hodgson wrote frantically on his notepad to keep up with everything the youngster had to say. Once they covered all the usual topics, Harry dropped the question he'd been waiting to ask, and Von answered.

"Yes, I enjoyed playing quarterback last year, but I'm happy to help the team in any way I can. We are off to another winning start, and that's all that matters."

"So, no hard feelings toward Reynolds Tichenor?" Harry asked.

"He's played well," Von complimented. He wasn't comfortable broaching the subject any further and turned the table on the reporter, "Say, why would you ask me such a personal question?"

"Readers today want more insight regarding the fellas who play and coach the game. They are no longer merely interested in the final score," Harry explained.

Von thought of his fascination for the Olympian, James Connolly, and understood.

"I'm not sure if you are aware, but people see you and others on the team as real-life heroes. Plus, humanizing the game helps to combat all the negative press that is swirling about regarding injuries and the like."

Von blushed, "Fair enough, Mr. Hodgson, but I'm no hero. And I'm sure your readers will be plenty interested in the score after our game with Virginia next week."

"No doubt, the Virginians will be the toughest opponent you've faced to date," Harry predicted. "Perhaps the toughest this school has *ever* faced. It's safe to say that most people expect your team will end up the underdog in that fight."

"Well, nobody *on our* team expects that. Or at least they'd better not," Von declared. "Say, are you familiar with the term, 'grit,' Mr. Hodgson?"

Harry nodded.

"Would you say that this team has grit? Do you think *I've* got grit?"

"Absolutely," Harry affirmed. "You all have it, and I just might make mention of that in my article."

Von asked Hodgson if he was familiar with the account of David and Goliath from the Bible, at which he responded in the affirmative.

"I think God blessed David with grit," Von stated. "Don't you worry, sir, we'll make sure you have a memorable story to write next week. Just like David and Goliath."

* * *

After escorting his parents to the rail station, Von returned to his room in Old College to freshen up from the game. After a wipe-down with a wash-cloth, he dashed on some cologne and put on a pair of clean trousers and a light sweater.

By this time the sun had moved half-way below the pines, but there was still enough light and warmth outside for him to grab a book and catch up on a reading assignment that he'd fallen behind on. Von headed out onto the campus courtyard, which was a popular place for students to study on nice days. Although sitting alone, he found the surroundings a bit distracting.

The triumphant sounds of students ringing the Chapel Bell resonated from over by the Athletic Field, which had become commonplace following each victory. A brass band could also be heard playing what sounded like *The Battle Hymn of the Republic* somewhere close by. It should havc been a night to celebrate a big win with everyone else, Von thought, but after a long week of practice, he had little time to finish his novel before Monday's class.

Despite everything going on around him, Von hunkered down and immersed himself into the pages of *Great Expectations*. He became so entranced that he failed to hear or see the assailants that snuck up from behind.

A rag wrapped his head and covered his mouth, which muted his screams. Next, a scratchy burlap seed bag came down, blinding his view. Quickly, his attackers lifted Von to his feet and lassoed a rope around his waist that kept him from squirming and also allowed them to pull him along.

They forced him to take steps in the direction of their choosing. Unable to maintain their silence, both muggers burst out laughing. With that, Von was no longer alarmed, but just plain angry.

He tried to holler out cries for help and shouted insults toward his kidnappers, but no avail. He wiggled and fought for freedom, but two against one with a bag over his head and a rope around his body proved to be too much, and he eventually surrendered to their will.

After what seemed like close to an hour-long stumble, Von was instructed to stand in place. He felt the warmth from and heard the distinctive sound of a crackling fire in front of him. The smell of smoke passed through his nostrils and into his lungs. Von could also hear mumbled voices and many footsteps rustling about, along with the occasional clanking sound of glass or copper.

Still, no one said a word to him. That is until they yanked the rope away and lifted the bag up and off of Von's head.

There, surrounding a bonfire before him, were Walter and the rest of his SAE fraternity brothers. There were also a handful of young ladies present, one of whom he recognized as the girl with those memorable green eyes that he'd seen at practice more than a year before. Together, the men broke out in a robust chorus of *For He's A Jolly Good Fellow* and lifted their glasses toward the unsuspecting guest of honor.

A round of applause came next, and Walter asked that Von say a few words. But all that came out were some unintelligible murmurs from beneath the towel that still covered his mouth. The group laughed as Von reached behind his head to untie the knot, and he was quickly assisted by Oliver, one of his captors.

Left awkwardly on the spot, Von managed to blurt out some words of appreciation but was still confused regarding the occasion. Walter explained that the party was for him; to celebrate their great triumph over "Those cheating bastards from Atlanta!" He went on to declare Von as the greatest Georgia man to have ever played the game, and everyone lifted their glass again.

Walter stepped forward and threw his arm around Von's shoulder, "I wasn't going to let you bury your face in some old boring book on what should be one of the greatest nights of your life!"

Von was grateful for his friend's intentions, but shook his head and announced, "I appreciate you fellas kidnapping me and all – I think – and throwing this shindig for me, but I've got to get through that Dickens book before Monday, or else."

Walter slurped from his mug, draped his arm over Von's shoulder, and proceeded to lead him away from the fire, "Or else what?" he asked, followed by a belch.

Von released himself from underneath Walter's hold and faced him, "Or else I could be on thin ice with my professor. And my mother."

Walter frowned, but cheered himself up with another taste of his drink.

"Besides," Von continued, "starting Monday we'll be going non-stop all week preparing for Virginia."

"That's just it, brother," Walter countered, "all you've got is tonight to have some fun. Forget about Charles Dickens for now and let yourself go a little. Besides, you've got all day tomorrow to read."

Von was tempted. It had been a great win, and everyone in town was celebrating — everyone except him.

Oliver walked up carrying two drinks and handed one to Von, exclaiming, "Great win, pal! I want you to chug this brew with me, right now! It will help you loosen up. Whaddaya say?"

Von accepted the cup and looked down at the froth inside of it. Oliver lifted his glass toward him with eyebrows raised.

In a flustered tone, Von handed the cup back to Oliver and forced, "Nah, fellas. I'm sorry, but I can't."

Both Walter and Oliver refuted his decision.

"I've gotta keep my head straight, and boozing up sure won't help me do that," Von protested. "I've got school work to do and a tough game coming up. Beating Tech is great, but beating the Virginians will be even greater. They are considered to be the best team in the South, so if we win, I guess that crown goes to us."

This time it was Oliver who took Von under his arm and pointed to the girl with green eyes, "You see that pretty gal over there?"

Von nodded, his eyes now locked on her.

"Her name is Viola, and she's had a crush on you ever since you arrived in Athens," Oliver informed. "If you're not going to drink with us tonight, then I suggest you do the next best thing and go talk to her. And if you play your cards right, I bet you'll be in for a few more surprises tonight."

"I don't know, Ollie," Walter interrupted. "Von's got a girl back home."

"Who asked 'ya?" Oliver charged. He put his attention back on Von and revealed, "She only agreed to come here tonight because we promised that you would be here. And whaddaya know, here you are. All you have to do is ask."

At that moment, Viola turned and looked in Von's direction, and they made instant eye-contact. The orange glow from the fire reflected off her deep, green eyes, and she offered up a smile that some might have deemed seductive.

Despite another warning from Walter, Von suddenly found himself standing alongside Viola at the fire. Alone.

They engaged in small talk for about ten minutes, initially about that day's game and football in general. Viola went on to explain that she was a student at Lucy Cobb, and whenever possible attended practice and home games to watch Von play.

"I'd love to go and see one of those wild games over in Atlanta," she purred. "I hear you've got another one coming up next Saturday."

Von confirmed and described their upcoming opponent: how big and fast they were, and how they had played three times as many games as Georgia in recent years.

"Most of our guys just don't have a lot of playing time; including me quite frankly," Von shared. "Our lack of experience in itself will be a tough factor for us to overcome."

Viola put her lips to Von's ear, and her warm breath felt good as she whispered, "Well, I for one don't care if you're experienced or not, Von." She took his hand and led him away from the fire to a more secluded place in the woods where they sat for a while.

Over the next few minutes, the two gazed into one another's eyes. They remained silent, except a few flirtatious giggles from Viola.

Finally, Von squeezed her hand and said, "You're a very pretty girl, Viola. Any boy would be crazy not to be attracted you, including me."

Not certain where he was going, Viola returned a look of confusion.

"But the thing is, I've got a girl back home. Her name is Emily, and if you met her, I think you'd like her."

Viola released his hand and stared at the ground, considering whether to fight for him or just let it go. She made her decision once Von spoke again.

"After the Virginia game I'm going to ask for her hand in marriage," Von disclosed. "I am in love with her."

With a sweet smile, Viola surrendered, "That's wonderful. And she's quite lucky to have found someone like you."

"Problem is the game is a week away, and I haven't even asked her father for his blessing yet," Von confessed.

"Don't fret; I'm sure he'll be proud to have you as his son-in-law."

"I'm not so sure," Von contested, "it's been hard enough getting my own father's blessing."

With a wink and a kiss to his cheek, Viola led Von to his feet and walked him back to the fire.

# HAIL MARY

*Do you remember that I woke in such a fuss that night, Rosie? Cold sweat running down my brow and my heart beating out of my chest? My first inclination was to jump on the first train to Atlanta in the morning and yank Von out of that lineup.*

*But I woke to what I believed to be sounder judgment. It was only a dream, right? I should have respected my dream.*

LITTLE FIVE POINTS, ATLANTA, GA
SATURDAY, OCTOBER 30, 1897

'Little Five Points' was an area of town where many electric streetcar routes converged and offered continued service to most parts of metropolitan Atlanta, which was becoming a very modern city for the Deep South.

In the early morning hours before the Georgia - Virginia matchup, frenzied fans were out in force, jockeying for a place in the trolley line. Management had already put as many cars on the Brisbane Park line as possible, but the wait times to get on one were still pushing an hour. Police working the scene did everything they could to direct pedestrian and horse traffic, help manage the trolley car queues, and keep the general peace.

Accompanied by Emily and her father Ira, Monty and Jack Pierce had arrived in Atlanta the night prior. Even with the pending transportation hassles ahead of them, they chose to enjoy a nice breakfast together at the hotel.

After their meal, the foursome waited in the trolley line for about fifty minutes before hopping on a car with a bunch of other people who were also wearing red and black colored outfits. Some onboard donned Virginia colors, but they were definitely in the minority and could do nothing but sit and listen to the cheers of the Georgia faithful all the way down the rails.

*Razzelty! Dazzelty!*
*Sis Boom Ah!*
*Georgia! Georgia!*
*Rah! Rah! Rah!!*

Their train car pulled up slowly behind a line of others waiting to unload outside the gates of Brisbane Park. After a short while, Monty and friends were dropped off in the middle of yet another mob scene. And the ceaseless chanting had only increased in volume and gusto.

It was gameday. The student newspaper in Athens, aptly named *The Red and Black*, had written that this contest was “Without a doubt the greatest athletic event that has ever occurred in the South.”

But not everyone present was a fan. A small group of picketers had assembled near the entry to protest football and ‘educate’ attendees about the inherent dangers that players risked suffering.

Something other than the protestors caught Emily's fancy, and she tugged at her father's shirtsleeve, "Look, Daddy, look!"

"What, sweetie? Where?" Ira asked with head pivoting from side to side.

"Three cars down," Emily pointed. "Why, it's the governor himself!"

Sure enough, Georgia Governor William Yates Atkinson was exiting a trolley labeled V.I.P. just a short distance away. The top man in the state had black wavy hair, which was complemented by a thick, black handlebar mustache. They watched as he assisted Mrs. Atkinson out of the car. She was a real beauty; a tall brunette sporting fiery red lipstick and a black Gainsborough hat.

"How about that," Emily said dreamily, "the governor and governess of Georgia at a football game! At *our* football game!"

"And they couldn't have picked a better one to attend," Jack commented.

Monty remarked, "I suppose I'm not all that surprised. He is, after all, an alumnus of the University."

"His wife is beautiful," Emily stated.

"Yes indeed," Jack agreed, "and I hope that she will be in full view from our seats."

Monty nudged his friend, "Don't forget there's a football contest to be played today, Jack."

"And what a tough ticket to get," Jack replied. "Football frenzy is surely at an all-time high."

Monty fiddled through his coat pockets for those treasured tickets as the foursome entered the main queue.

"Thank you for inviting my father and me along to see Von play," Emily expressed. "This will be Daddy's first football game."

"You are welcome," Monty returned, "but it was my parents who gave up their seats for the two of you." He directed his next comment toward Ira, "Von has been anxious to have you out to a game, and I expect he intends on making this one extra special."

"Well, I'm much obliged, and the feeling is mutual. I've been looking forward to this all week!"

* * *

Von stared down at the heart made of yarn that he held in his hands. He began to squeeze it in rhythm with his real heart that pound inside of his chest. The entire team sat quietly around him inside the Red and Black dressing room as they patiently waited for their coach to join them.

Despite the team's stillness, it was still noisy.

Thousands of footsteps tromped about in the grandstands above their heads. A marching band tooted their horns and banged their drums out on the lawn. Fans behind all four walls were heard cheering and jeering at the top of their lungs – and the game had not yet begun.

Waiting with the players were Cow Nalley, Thomas Reed, Dr. Charles Herty, and a few other faculty members. Reed anxiously checked his pocket watch every ninety seconds or so.

Finally, Coach McCarthy blast through the door just as a rousing rendition of Sousa's *Stars and Stripes Forever* began playing outside. He ran his fingers through his hair, took a deep breath, and addressed the team.

"Listen up, men!" he hollered. "I am a Yankee!"

The team looked around at each other, dumbfounded.

McCarthy repeated, "Come on, I know you all heard me. I am a Yankee! And a *damned* old Yankee at that!"

Not knowing how they were supposed to react, some of the players countered his declaration with some lighthearted boos.

"Yes, yes, I know," he conceded, "but just remember who won the war!" he exclaimed playfully, leading to increased boos and scattered laughter. He continued, "My point is, collegiate football in this country started up North – by Yankees like myself – and thus the teams up there enjoy the advantage of experience and still dominate our sport. Did you know that the people at Princeton, Yale, Cornell and the like regard our quality of play as second rate?"

Hisses. Cat-calls. And more boos.

"Well gentlemen, with a win today, we have a chance to make a statement. A statement not only for U of G, but for the advancement of football across the entire Deep South. But it won't come easy. Nothing worth doing ever does," he assured. "Last year, you conquered those beasts from North Carolina. But the team we face today is much stronger than even they, and dare I say as talented as one of those northern squads. Why, I hear the average weight of these Virginians is one-fifty-five! That's at least five, maybe ten, more pounds than us on aggregate."

McCarthy glanced over at Reynolds, "But take little 'ole Tick as an example of bravery. He can't be more than one-twenty soaking wet, but he won't let the physical size of an opponent intimidate him! Hell, I hear all the time about how he bucked straight up to Cow back in ninety-six. There's no fear in him! And there should be no fear in any of you, either," he dared while scanning the room.

Every eye in the place was locked onto Coach McCarthy as he pointed toward one of the walls, "In the opposing dressing room –

right over in that other wing of this stadium – Coach Bergen and the Cavaliers await what they think will be another easy victory." He paused to waggle his finger and claimed, "Well, the element of surprise is in our favor, boys. Little do the Virginians know that today, they'll line up against what is truly the best football club in the South!"

The team erupted in cheers.

"Let's send a message that collegiate football is played best in Georgia!"

They continued to yell louder and louder.

"This is our day!" McCarthy cried over their screams. "Let's beat Virginia!"

The men hollered loud and long. Coach Nalley directed them into a single-file line to follow behind Thomas Reed and his stick, and they streamed out of the room and into the sunlight, chanting in unison,

*Hoo-rah-rah!*
*Hoo-rah-rah!*
*Rah-rah-Georgia!*

Gammon and Tichenor shared an awkward glance toward one another before falling in the back of the line.

* * *

Well into the first half, the Cavaliers possessed the ball just in front of their own goal line.

"Watch the left halfback boys!" shouted Gammon from his middle linebacker position. "Hold 'em here, and we'll have great field position coming back!"

Von eyeballed his team captain Kent, who was flanked to his right, and directed him, "You've got to keep your eye on that halfback, Billy. He's been busting through our line all day."

Kent returned a nod of confidence.

The teams squared up at the line of scrimmage, shoulder to shoulder, chin to chin. Walsh, the Virginia quarterback, hollered out his cadence.

Walsh accepted the snap of the ball and handed it to Julien Hill, the left halfback who'd been busting through the line. A hole opened at the tackle position, and once again he ran through it with great speed.

Kent managed to wiggle free from his opponent and fell to his right. With outstretched arms, he barely got one hand around one of Hill's ankles – just enough to trip him up.

The ball carrier struggled to stay on his feet but still managed to keep his focus on the line to make a first down ahead. From behind, Gammon skirted a blocker, dove low and wrapped his arms around the runner's legs. Unable to keep running, Hill fell chest first into the ground.

The jarring impact with the turf jarred the ball loose, but after a frenzied scramble Hill was able to regain possession, albeit a yard short of a first down.

On the sideline, a frustrated Coach Nalley hopped around and cursed out loud. Failing to capitalize on a possible turnover that close to the opponent's goal line was a huge missed opportunity, and he knew it.

Reed and many others were also discouraged by the outcome, so Coach McCarthy tried to cool heads, "That's alright, fellas," he assured while motioning for them to calm down with his hands, "It's third down. We're still going to get the ball back and will be headed downhill."

He spun toward the players on the field and hollered, "Take third down formations! Punt-three formation!"

After that, McCarthy searched the sidelines for a long and lanky fellow named Brooks Clarke, who the coach affectionately called Slim. At 6'4", Brooks wasn't hard to find. He towered above his other teammates, and he served a special purpose.

"We're running punt-three, Slim. Get out there and do your thing!" McCarthy ordered.

Both teams had already begun taking their positions as Clarke hurried out to the right side of the defensive line. Von counted heads and noticed one too many.

"It's punt-three! Punt-three!" he shouted even louder. "Price, get off the field. Brooks is in!"

Fred was able to get off the field just one second before the ball was hiked, avoiding a penalty against the Red and Black.

Clarke manhandled his defender, and with an extraordinary shove grounded his opponent's backside against the gridiron. There was nothing in between him and the Virginia kicker.

Harried by the oncoming pressure, the punter was off his mark and launched a low kick. Rushing in, Clarke stretched out his long arms and clipped the ball with his fingers, spinning it end-over-end and straight up in the air.

At least five or six men touched it before it fell back to earth. From there, it bounced in several directions by way of touch or kick.

Eventually, Billy Kent fell on the loose object behind the Virginia goal line.

Touchdown, Georgia!

Immediately after, the marching band struck a stirring tune. Fans went berserk. The wooden grandstands shook and swayed. And Monty's group celebrated with them all.

"Six-to-four now with a chance for us to tie it up on this conversion!" Monty hollered. He did a double-take toward the field and reported, "Seems that Tichenor is in for the kick and not Von."

Back on the field, the teams lined up, and Reynolds prepared to attempt the kick. Since Kent had fallen on the ball on a far side of the field, it was a very awkward angle to the goalposts and was sure to be a challenging try.

Tichenor nodded ready, and the ball was snapped. When kicked, it crossed the goal line but sailed wide of the post — no good.

The miss let a little air out of the collective Georgia balloon. Monty and his gang were certainly disappointed.

"Why did they let that Auburn fellow kick?" Emily protested. "They should've had Von kick it!"

A nearby stranger with a scraggly red beard and rosy cheeks yapped back, "You gotta admit, young lady, that was a rude angle. Even Gammon would have had a tough time with that one!"

Emily was quick to counter, "Oh hush, you half-wit! Von makes that kick nine times out of ten!"

Her adversary disagreed with a shake of his head but went back to minding his own business.

As play moved further into the first half, Virginia lined up to attempt a field goal. A successful kick would stretch their lead to seven points.

Clarke was in again at right defensive end, anxiously wiggling his fingers and staring at the ball under center as he tried to anticipate the snap.

Von stood several yards behind the line, ready to run forward and leap up and over the offensive line for a shot at interfering with the flight of the kick.

Snap. Kick. Good!

The ball sailed just inside the goal post for a five-point score. Many bodies watched the end-result of the play with their backs on the ground — most of those being Georgia players.

The Cavaliers were quick to get up and scampered off the field, while some members of the Red and Black were slow and lethargic. But not Gammon.

"What are you slugs doing?" Von challenged. "Get up! Up on your feet!" he ordered with a raised voice.

Still on his back, Fred Price wailed, "Let up, Gammon. Perhaps this isn't our day to make that statement."

Von was outraged by the comment.

"Not our day?!" he cried out while circling Price's body. "Not our day?! There's a whole 'nother half left in this game, Fred! And I know there's gotta be at least that much left in you – in all of us!" he charged while surveying his teammates.

Captain Billy weighed in, "Fred, do as Von says and pick your rear off the ground. Eleven to four is not insurmountable."

Price sat up and raised his hand to Billy for help, but after a shake of the head was left sitting on the field alone as the rest of his team hopped on their feet and took off for the sideline.

Fred pulled himself up and followed behind, passing an opponent on the way.

"Had enough, lunkhead?" asked the Virginian.

His blood pressure on the rise, Price responded, "I've got my eyes on you, and I'm gonna knock your teeth right out of that trap of yours before this day is over with."

The Virginian smiled widely at Fred, and in doing so opened his mouth and exposed two already missing front teeth.

"Sorry, loser, but somebody already beat you to that, too!" he smarted.

On the ensuing kickoff, Price received the ball. He ran left. He ran right. But there was no hole to scamper through. In the corner of his eye, Fred spotted the fleet-footed Tick on his left and tossed the ball in that direction just as tacklers brought him down.

Surprised, but alert, Tichenor swiped the ball from out of the air and sped off into the open field.

Seeing the play unfold from the grandstands, Monty and friends were on their feet, watching with dropped jaws as Reynolds ran uphill.

"Run little man," Jack Pierce pled from afar, "run, Tick, run!"

And that's exactly what he did. Run.

With eyes squarely focused on the goal line, Tick ran as fast as he could. But as he neared the opposing twenty-five-yard line, Reynolds felt an unfamiliar feeling. He was winded. And slowing down.

The muffled sounds of more than a thousand cheering fans reminded him that people depended on him to score. Uncharacteristic of Tichenor, he broke sight of the goal and turned to assess the position of the enemy. Worry set in as he saw a large-framed Virginian, with two missing teeth, closing in fast.

That worry changed to delight as Reynolds noticed Von speeding in a direct angle toward the would-be tackler. A smile stretched across Tick's face, and a second-wind kicked in.

But as Von got within a yard or two of his rival, his feet crossed one another and tripped him up. The ensuing fall stirred a cloud of dust.

The Virginian aptly crashed down upon Tichenor's much smaller frame, smashing the runner's face into the grass and dirt below. Tick rolled on his backside, grimacing in pain and holding his shoulder.

Von recovered and ran to help, along with another teammate who had caught up from behind. The pair lifted Reynolds to his feet, who was still grasping his shoulder and now hobbling on a bad ankle.

Coach McCarthy hollered out to all his men and waved them toward the sideline. Nalley was by his side and visibly upset, kicking up dust and cursing up a storm. Both coaches grew impatient as they waited for the slow-moving Tichenor and his escorts to arrive.

"Get in here, men!" McCarthy ordered as they limped onto the sideline and joined the rest. "Listen up! Tick looks like he's going to be out for a play or two." He turned toward Cow and instructed, "Nalley, put Cox in for this next offensive series until Tick has a chance to catch his breath."

"But Cox ain't no quarterback, Coach."

McCarthy shook his head, "I know that. Put him in at fullback for Heaven's sake. Gammon will move to quarterback. He knows what to do."

That notion angered Nalley, and he barked back, "Dangit, Coach! Gammon bailed from that block on purpose! He left Tick out there for the kill!"

Von stepped forward to defend himself, but Cow held a hand in his face and kept complaining, "I saw it, and I'm sure the rest of these boys saw it! It was plain as day!"

McCarthy tried to diffuse the conflict and spoke to the entire group, "We are down a man, and that means everyone must assume more responsibility from here on out. Georgia men don't quit!"

There were a few 'rah-rahs' from the circle.

"We're in great field position here," he continued. "With Gammon behind center, we'll run our basic rushing formations. It's a good opportunity to chip into the lead before intermission." With a glance toward Cow, he advised, "But we've got to stay united and play as a team. We cannot let anything or anyone divide us now. Take your positions!"

The huddle broke and the offense trotted out onto the field, where the Cavaliers were already waiting for them. Losing Tichenor to injury was not how Von had expected or wanted to retake the quarterback position, but he was eager to get behind center and take a snap. He took deep and deliberate breaths to try and keep his mind from racing. Once again, he felt his chest beating rapidly, which for a moment made him think of his heart-shaped pin cushion back in the dressing room, which made him think of Emily, which made him think of Ira, which made him think of the pending question to be asked following the game.

"Von!" shouted Billy Kent while motioning for him to pick up the pace. "Snap out of it!"

Von had drifted off and was embarrassed. He was also bothered by the sensation of a burning stare coming from his backside. A quick peek behind and a double-take at Cow identified the heat source.

* * *

Unfortunately, the Red and Black failed to capitalize on the good field position and left the field trailing 11-4 at halftime. Inside the dressing room, a gassed team listened to McCarthy's rousing speech – probably his best one yet as a young coach. Cow added some dramatic effect by pounding his fists on just about every inanimate object in the room.

A horn blew outside signaling both teams to return. The U of G players stood and took their place in a single-file line, with Reed again at the helm. But during this march, there were no exuberant cheers from the team. They filed out of the room in eerie silence.

Once onto the field, the Georgia faithful bellowed and hollered with great enthusiasm at the top of their lungs. They held onto all hopes that their heroes would play better in the second half.

Georgia opened it by kicking off, and after both squads swapped possession several times, the score remained unchanged. After receiving a punt, Virginia had the ball again and driving toward mid-field.

It had been a hard-fought contest. Players on both teams were sweaty, dirty, bruised, and bloodied by cuts and scratches. Their hair was filthy. But battle conditions were taking a noticeably greater toll on the smaller squad from Athens.

The Georgia defensive unit waited for the next play to begin. They stood with hands on hips, sucking in as much of the crisp autumn air as their lungs would allow. Even Von bent over and placed his hands on his knees, gasping for some much-needed oxygen.

From his crouched position, he pushed, “Alright, men. Time to make another stand.”

Billy was concerned about Von’s physical appearance and asked how he was feeling.

“Don’t worry about me, Billy,” he snapped back with a brazen glare.

“It’s just you don’t look so good to me. We’ve all been playing hard, but you’ve been in on every single down. Maybe you ought to sit out a few.”

“If they score again, we lose. A Georgia man never quits.” Von reminded his captain.

The time for chatter was over as Virginia took their positions on the line of scrimmage. The defense hurried into place. Walsh began to holler out signals. Players on both sides tried to focus on him as the delirious sounds of screaming fans echoed inside their skulls.

The ball was snapped and Walsh immediately tossed it to the halfback, Hill, whose eyeballs enlarged as he frantically searched for another hole to run through.

Gammon studied the developments from behind the line. As Hill made a move to his left, Von countered by moving to his right.

To avoid a couple of bodies that had fallen in his path, Hill made a quick side-step and ran further to his left. But that didn’t prove much better, as what seemed to be the entire left side of the line came collapsing toward him. The falling shoulder of a defensive player struck the back side of Hill’s knee, causing him to lose balance and stumble.

Impressively, the runner stuck out an arm and managed to right himself back onto his feet. And now there was no one in front of him.

Unseen by Hill, Gammon soared in low and like a torpedo. But unfortunately, Von missed his mark and merely clipped the runner's thigh as he shot by, barely impeding Hill's forward progress.

With no energy lost, Von continued his flight down and into the turf, striking chin first and with much force. His head was thrust backward in a violent twist. Beads of sweat flew from his thick head of hair.

A couple of Georgia players chased after Hill and eventually tackled him about twenty yards downfield. Others near the original line of scrimmage struggled to untangle themselves from the limbs of their opponents.

Von lay motionless on the ground.

An umpire blew his whistle and tried to help separate several clumps of squirming bodies. Each man rose to his feet, except Von. Billy was the first to notice and kneeled next to him.

Kent placed a hand on Von's shoulder and shook it, "Hey, buddy. Are you all right? Dangit, I told you to sit one out!" After no response, he pled, "Hey, Gammon . . . get up! You hurt or what?"

Fred Price now stood over Von and quipped, "Thought you said Georgia men don't quit, Gammon."

Still out from his injury, Reynolds watched from his seat on the sideline bench; his old Auburn vest tucked comfortably under his buns. He tried to get a glimpse of his fallen teammate but couldn't see through the circle of players that had surrounded him.

"Who's down?" he asked aloud.

"It's Gammon," Nalley confirmed, standing close by on the sideline. "Probably knocked the wind out of himself. You know him; he'll be up on his feet in a jiffy."

Tichenor felt uneasy. A full minute passed with no one doing anything to help Von, so he decided to act. Despite an appeal from Nalley to stay seated, Reynolds left the sideline and hobbled out onto the field. Once at the scene of the accident, he practically pushed Billy Kent out of the way and crouched down on his knees next to Von.

Reynolds asked Von if he could hear him, but there was no response. He repeated the question, this time with a slight shake of Von's arm, but still nothing.

"Come on, man . . . answer me, dammit!" Reynolds cried in frustration.

Alas, an eye opened. Partially. Von looked up at Tick as best he could but remained speechless. His lips began to quiver as if laying in an icebox — a trickle of blood leaked from one of his nostrils.

At that, Reynolds stood and glared at the officials. "Hey gents, we need some help out here," he said with some urgency in his voice.

The referees looked at one another but said or did nothing. The inaction elevated Tick's intensity.

"You've both made it obvious out here today that you are blind, but are you also deaf?!" he exclaimed. "I said we need some help out here . . . of the medical variety!"

From afar, Monty stretched his long neck and peered through a pair of field glasses to identify the injured player.

"Well, Monty, who is it?" asked Pierce.

"I cannot tell," Monty replied, "there are too many standing in the way."

Back on the field, one of the officials finally signaled to the sideline for assistance, prompting a policeman to jot out with Coach Nalley by his side.

Tick decided to try and help Von sit up and began by raising his head, but the injured player began to vomit wildly. That caused most of the circle to back off immediately in disgust.

Reynolds, now covered in discharge, laid Von's head back down.

"He's lost all his color, fellas," Tick stated nervously. "Where is that doctor?"

As the policeman and Nalley stepped up, one of the officials declared, "Alright, gentlemen, vomit or not, you realize we're going to have to move this boy from the field and get this game back underway."

Without further haste, Nalley and Billy each took one end of the limp body and carried Von carefully toward the sideline. Tichenor staggered close behind, assisted by the policeman.

"Line 'em up boys, or darkness will be an issue soon," said the official.

Players on both sides refocused enough to line up and snap the next play, just as Von was laid on his back a few feet off of the gridiron.

It was Emily who first recognized the wounded player, and she gasped with hand over mouth. Her reaction said enough, but Monty peered through his glasses again to verify that it was indeed his younger brother.

Jack stood aghast.

"We must go down there!" Emily insisted while tugging at Monty's coat sleeve. "He must be hurt badly!"

"Hold on a minute," Jack reasoned, "if we go down, what on earth are we going to do when we get there?"

"More than I can do from up here," Monty stated before he charged through the row of patrons to his left. Emily was on his heels, with Jack and Ira anchoring the rear.

Attending the game as a spectator, Dr. Bizzell was summoned from his seat in the stands and answered the call. The game roared on nearby as he joined Cow, Reynolds, Billy, and the policeman – all hovering above Von's shaking body. The crowd, however, had turned their attention back on the field and cheered every play.

"Thanks for coming down, doctor," the policeman said.

After a quick inspection, Bizzell stated the obvious. "His appearance is not good," he relayed, "but let me see what I can do."

Presuming the doctor was now in control of things, McCarthy stepped over to break things up, "Alright, boys, let the good doctor take care of Von. I need Billy back on the field and Coach Nalley and Tick over by the bench with me."

After a nod, Billy conformed and ran back onto the field. Reynolds was not as quick to comply and remained by Von's side. His defiance did not sit well with the ball coach.

"Did you hear me, Tick?!" McCarthy growled. "Let the doctor do his work. The faster you get out of his way the sooner Gammon will be back on the field."

Reynolds faced him, "I don't think so, Coach. I don't think he's going back into this game." He kneeled beside Von and added, "Look at how violently he shakes."

Bizzell began searching through his medical bag while Reynolds placed a hand on Von's shoulder, hoping to comfort him. At least a little.

With arms held high in the air, McCarthy complained, “You and Gammon have left me with no qualified quarterback!”

Reynolds couldn’t believe the insensitive comment, and with much displeasure hopped up to begin his shuffle toward the bench.

“Is that all you’re concerned about, *Coach*?” he said to McCarthy in passing.

Nalley chimed in and offered, “Hey, Coach; I’ll stay here with Von. You get back to the ball game.”

After a deep breath, McCarthy nodded in the affirmative and followed behind Tichenor.

Leaning in, Nalley probed, “How bad is it really, doctor?”

Preparing a needle for injection, Bizzell answered, “This boy is in bad shape. Hopefully, some morphine will at least ease his pain.”

Even after the needle was inserted into Von’s chest, he showed no significant reaction.

Surprisingly, Tichenor soon reappeared and was holding his Auburn vest. Without permission from the doctor, he laid it on top of Von’s body. Almost instantly, the shivers began to slow.

“We must get this boy to a hospital,” Bizzell demanded. “Summon a carriage – and do it now.”

The policeman acknowledged the order and sped away, just as two Cavaliers overran the play that was occurring on the field. They tripped and fell uncontrollably out of bounds; coming to a stop less than eight feet from where Von lay.

Tichenor turned and woofed at them, “Back off you brutes! We’ve got a very sick man over here!”

The Virginians snarled back as if Tichenor and Gammon were the obstructions. Just then, Tick felt a slight tug on his sleeve. He peeked down to see Von looking up at him through eyes that were only partially open.

Von started to speak twice but struggled to get any words out. The doctor asked him to stay still and quiet and assured that help was on the way, but that didn't stop his efforts to communicate.

Reynolds leaned in closer. In a gruff whisper, Von slowly exhaled, "A Georgia man never quits."

That brought a little smile to Tick's face, and he encouraged, "I know, Von. I know."

"And I didn't quit . . . ," a cough broke Von's sentence. "And I didn't quit on you, either."

* * *

Dusk had set in as the game neared its final moments. Outside the park, Monty, Jack, Emily, and Ira watched as medical personnel placed Von into the carriage ambulance that was to carry him to Atlanta's Grady Hospital. With some assistance from the others, Tichenor climbed aboard to accompany him on the trip.

A sizeable crowd encircled the area around them. Some people were crying. Some prayed out loud, and some prayed silently. Ira held Emily close as she wept.

After the ambulance pulled away, a couple of men dressed in Virginia colors passed by, and one of them blurted at Emily, "Ahh, quit your crying, little lady. You'll get over it by morning."

The other snipped, "I don't know, Vernon? Seventeen to four is quite a rout. Might take her several days to get over this one!"

"And to think there was actually speak of an upset today!" the first man teased as they carried on their way, laughing.

* * *

GRADY HOSPITAL, ATLANTA, GA
LATER THAT NIGHT

Monty and his faction met Tichenor at the hospital. Walter and a few fraternity members who'd made the trip from Athens for the game were also there, all anxiously waiting in the hallway outside of Von's room for an update from the doctor.

"When did he tell you this again?" Monty asked Walter.

"It was Wednesday evening; after he'd returned from practice. I remember it distinctly because it was such an unusual thing for him to say."

"Agreed," Monty replied. "I've never known Von to be fearful of anybody. Or anything for that matter. I mean, maybe he has, but I've never heard him admit it out loud."

Walter clarified, "Let me rephrase. He never actually said that he was afraid of the Virginians, only that he was uneasy about the game for some reason. It was just a gut feeling that came over him."

Out front, Cow and most of the Red and Black team arrived, but they were delayed entry into the hospital because of a sudden influx of battered and bloodied people being rushed inside. Nalley asked a tending policeman what had happened.

It was explained that following the ball game, two trollies had collided head-on outside of the park. One, packed full of passengers leaving the game, had crested a hill and was picking up speed on the downslope when it slammed into an arriving car that was chugging up the other side. Although dark at the time of the accident, neither trolley had their headlights on.

And to make matters worse, another car trailing the first soon peaked the same hill and smashed into the rear of the already mangled wreckage. They brought the most severely injured to Grady, but due to the sheer numbers involved, those with lesser wounds were taken to nearby houses to wait for medical assistance.

Hearing all the commotion from down the hall, Monty made his way to the lobby and was the first to see Cow and the team as they entered the facility. Coach Nalley and Monty made eye contact, and without a word, Cow locked him in an embrace.

"This has been a tragic night, all the way around," Cow said upon releasing Von's brother. He enlightened Monty as to why so many others were being carted in, and they both overheard Grady staff announce that at least two of the trolley passengers had been pronounced dead on arrival.

At that, the strong man of Rome began to weep. Once again, Cow put an arm around to console him and assured that Von was going to be okay.

"He's a tough one, Monty," Cow asserted. "If anybody can pull through, it's your little brother."

Monty wiped a tear away from his cheek and composed himself with a nod. From down the hall, Walter hollered out for Monty to return.

The attending physician had surfaced from Von's room to give an update. Monty pulled up with the team in tow, and the doctor spoke, "I regret to report that Richard's condition is critical. He has a fractured skull, and his temperature has risen to one-hundred-nine degrees. Are there any family members present?"

All heads turned toward Monty.

"Yes doctor, I'm his brother; and our father is on his way from Rome as we speak. He caught the late train after hearing of the accident on the telegraph."

"And does the young man have a mother?" the doctor inquired.

"Yes, but she remains at home."

The doctor cleared his throat, "I'm afraid you'd best summon your mother as well."

At that, the doctor excused himself and departed down the hall to help handle the throngs of incoming patients. He'd left the door to Von's room open, and half of those waiting in the hall tried to rush in to see him.

An alert nurse inside the room held off the stampede and insisted that only two people come in at a time. Naturally, Monty and Emily were up first.

"Wait," Cow said to Emily before entering. He reached out and handed over the knitted heart, which he had retrieved from the dressing room at Brisbane. Her eyes swelled with gratitude.

Inside the room, they found that Von was without color and looked very frail as he lay with eyes closed in the bed. Hot and fevered, his thick hair was drenched with sweat. Emily could barely stand the sight and took hold of Monty's mid-section, sobbing out loud.

This time it was Monty who played consoler. He hugged her back and stated, "The doctor's job is done. Von is in God's hands now."

With the permission of the nurse, Emily took Von's hands and tearfully placed the heart between them.

Two-by-two the others took a turn bedside. Cow was the odd-man out and entered alone at the last. It was in those precious moments that he made his peace with Von.

# TIME EXPIRED

*It is the greatest tragedy of parents to witness the death of their child, and I did just that at three-forty-five the following morning while standing at Von's hospital bedside. Courageously, he mustered up enough grit to last until I could arrive and say my good-byes. And although you did not arrive until soon after, it is my whole-hearted belief that he felt your presence in that room before drifting into eternity.*

MYRTLE HILL CEMETERY, ROME, GA
MONDAY, NOVEMBER 1, 1897

Von was taken from this earth a little more than one month prior to his eighteenth birthday. One day later at just before noon, a large gathering of family and friends huddled around the gravesite that was marked with a modest headstone. However, the plot was located atop a hill that afforded a breathtaking view of the surrounding area. The closed casket was adorned with many beautiful flower arrangements, and a football signed by all of Von's teammates served as the centerpiece.

Emily and Walter stood behind the Gammon family, who sat in chairs alongside the casket. The entire U of G football team stood three rows deep on the opposite side, while other close friends and acquaintances filled the gaps and spaces on both ends and all around. Even a few members of the Virginia football squad, including Head Coach Martin Bergen, delayed their trip back home to attend the service. The turnout demonstrated an outpouring of love, support, and sorrow for Von and his family.

Reverend Geotschius of the First Presbyterian Church presided, "There is no grief in Heaven, for life is but one glad day. There is no death in Heaven, for they who gain that shore have won their immortality through Jesus Christ, and can die no more. Amen."

The crowd repeated "Amen" as one.

The minister approached the parents and spoke with them quietly. They both nodded, and Rosalind stood to give Geotschius a hug of appreciation.

When he moved on to comfort other family members, Rosalind caught a glimpse of Cow, who'd stepped forward and lifted the football off the casket. Nalley looked her way, and they made eye contact.

With a solemn face, Cow kissed the ball and held it out in her direction before placing it back into position. The action was repeated next by Reynolds, then one-by-one each member of the Red and Black football team followed suit.

When the graveside service came to a close, the crowd stirred and mingled about the area. Some wished the family final condolences or offered one last farewell to Von before the casket was lowered into the ground. Sporadic, almost tearful-like, drops of rain began to fall.

Out of respect, the men from Virginia had remained off to the side and somewhat distant from the rest of the gathering. As they began to leave the site, several men from Rome approached from behind.

"Hey Coach . . . Coach Bergen!" one of the men shouted toward the Cavaliers.

The coach turned just as a clap of thunder sounded above, and the local man started in on him, "You and your boys there got a lotta nerve showin' up here today."

The Virginia team stepped quickly to stand guard in front of their coach, but Bergen held out his arms on both sides to hold them back.

"I'm sorry, mister, but I didn't catch your name," the coach responded.

Dark grey clouds had blocked out the sun, and angry skies rumbled high above their heads.

"Name don't matter none, I speak for the town," he replied. "Matter fact, I speak for the entire state of Georgia. Your foul play on Saturday cost this boy his life, and left a grieving mother in your wake."

Bergen took a look around. Other folks had begun to converge in on the conversation, so he wanted to consider his next words carefully.

Drawn toward the discussion, Tichenor strolled over and stood beside the local men, but spoke to the coach, "Is there a problem here, Coach Bergen?"

"These gentlemen are of the opinion that my team played dirty on Saturday, and they're none too pleased about it."

McCarthy noticed Tick's locale and sensed another storm brewing on the ground. He skipped over and also addressed his colleague, "Martin, it was a nice gesture for you and the fellows to attend the service today."

One of the other local men broke in, "Don't patronize these swindlers! They came down here with no other intent than to cheat, maim and destroy, and we aim to hold them accountable. Right here and right now!"

McCarthy held an open palm toward the three, "Hold on a moment, sir. Coach Bergen and his team had nothing to do with Von's misfortune."

The raindrops thickened and began to increase in number, but no one moved an inch.

"You're not gonna stand up for your own man?" the local challenged. "What kind of a *coach* are you, McCarthy?"

Another man from Rome reminded his buddy, "You know he ain't from around here neither. McCarthy's a Yankee! I looked that up. Hell, none of 'em ain't nothin' more than two-bit rotten Yanks!"

The local trio and the two coaches exchanged stares and glares.

The Cavalier quarterback, Walsh, snickered before chiming in, "Wait a minute; don't you three fools know that Virginia fought on the side of the Rebs?"

Bergen instructed Walsh and the rest of his team to stay out of it.

Tichenor attempted to diffuse, "Listen, you gents are simply mistaken. What happened to Von was clearly an accident."

One of the men snapped at Reynolds, "Well as long as we's choosin' sides I believe you ain't from around these parts neither, ya' yella' bellied traitor!"

Bergen declared, "Let's all slow it down before things get out of hand. We're on sacred ground, after all. Show some reverence."

All eyes were on the Virginia coach as he continued, "The game was played clean. Hard played yes, but not rough or foul. Our men had been instructed to play fairly and did so. You have my word on the fact that I saw no hitting at all; and no kneeing or such work."

"Your word?" one of the men interrupted. "Why we 'sposed to take ya' on just your word?"

Monty had snuck up from behind and commanded, "Hey, mister. Why don't you pipe down and let the coach speak?"

The local posse seemed to respect Monty's authority and gave the floor back to Bergen, who explained, "Gammon was hurt when we had the ball, attempting to tackle Hill over there." He pointed at the halfback, Julien. "This precludes any probability that we are to blame. The play in question was straight formation. No tricks."

The rain slowed to a sprinkle, inviting more people who'd been waiting under tree branches to circle the argument.

Monty testified, "I for one know what a zealous player Von was." He paused to wipe a tear from his cheek but chuckled at the same time. "My little brother was always jumping in one pile or another, doing everything he could for his team. He simply took one leap too many."

The local men glanced at one another and backed down from their aggressive positions.

As they moved away, Tichenor stepped toward Bergen and exclaimed, "The Virginians have no blood on their hands. Monty is right; Von always played hard, either with me or against me. And sometimes, unfortunate as it is, the harder you play, the harder you fall." He paused to clear his throat before announcing, "No one at school was better liked than Von, and his death has brought sadness to all of us. I for one am done playing football. For good. And I'm glad to hear that the University was wise enough to cancel our remaining schedule."

Von's parents had been listening from a distance. J.A. handed his wife a handkerchief to wipe the mixture of tears and rain pellets from her face.

The debate over football was not isolated to Von's memorial service. Not in the least. That very afternoon it continued all the way up the steps of the Georgia Capitol building in Atlanta and into the legislative chambers.

During the fall of 1896, twenty-six young men across the country were reported to have died from afflictions attributed to playing football. In the spring of '97, a bill to abolish the game in Georgia by making it an illegal activity had failed in the State Legislature. Von's tragedy, however, gave new life to the measure and it was quickly reintroduced, this time with fervent support in the State House. Lawmakers tasted blood and were out to kill the game.

The proposed resolution forbade the game to be played at any state-run institution or facility. Also, anyone found guilty of playing the sport would be subject to a misdemeanor charge and a $25 fine.

Georgia Tech and Mercer wasted no time and elected to abide by the pending law and immediately disbanded their football teams. Multiple colleges and universities, some even outside of Georgia, followed their example and did the same. Several state governments around the country jumped on board and introduced similar legislation.

Almost overnight, Richard Vonalbade Gammon had become the poster-boy for the anti-football movement. And it was picking up steam.

* * *

*On Wednesday, only a few days after Von's passing, we traveled to Atlanta along with Monty and Nellie to witness the House vote as special guests of the governor. This included reserved viewing seats in the chamber balcony, train fare, and two hotel rooms – all compliments of the state.*

*I recall that many other folks from around the region, either for or against the measure, flocked into town. It was, in itself, a game-like atmosphere.*

GEORGIA CAPITOL BUILDING, ATLANTA, GA
WEDNESDAY, NOVEMBER 3, 1897

Hundreds of people, maybe even a thousand, milled around outside the Capitol on the morning of the House vote. Newspaper boys pedaled their wares to passersby featuring headlines such as *DEATH KNELL OF FOOTBALL*.

Rumors were spreading amongst the crowd that a man in England had been arrested for manslaughter after afflicting a fatal blow upon his opponent during a football match. This was serious stuff.

As the Gammon clan arrived on the scene, they noticed an impromptu 'press conference' unfolding on the steps leading up to the main entrance and scurried over to listen. Monty recognized Charles Herty at the top-step, flanked by Thomas Reed. Many reporters and bystanders stood below.

Herty began, "I was responsible for the emergence of football at U of G. As an undergraduate nearly fifteen years ago, no one knew or spoke of the game. Later, I learned about it and fell in love with the sport as a graduate student at Johns Hopkins. When I returned to Athens in the fall of 1891 to instruct chemistry, there was but a crude field on which to play, mostly made of dirt and rocks."

The fairly amusing comment sparked some chuckles from those present.

"With a ball and a rule book," Herty explained, "I recruited a group of young men to take a chance and join one of the very first football clubs south of Raleigh. And despite contending with the poorest equipment in the region, our squad managed an undefeated season within five years of inception. This past winter, a proud group of Georgia alumni raised enough money to grade and seed our old dirt field and install a new set of bleachers."

A respectful silence surrounded Herty as he paused to collect his thoughts. When ready, he related, "Football has won the hearts of thousands, and I predict it will only continue to gain popularity in the next century."

He removed a couple of torn-out newspaper pages from his coat pocket.

"I'd like to read excerpts from two articles that appeared in the papers yesterday," Charles announced before clearing his throat and adjusting his reading glasses. "The Georgia – Virginia game has awakened the attention of the public to the outrage which should have been stamped out long ago. It is not a game, but a fierce contest and combat upon the field with but few or none of the expected elements in which the rules of football describe. Under no view or consideration, whatsoever, can this modern-day dangerous, brutal, and savage football contest be justified or excused."

He looked up from the story, and a good number of people in attendance cheered, prompting Reed to step forward in debate mode. But he honored Dr. Herty's request and stood down.

"Here is another," he continued. "Football is worse than hazing and prizefighting, both of which are prohibited at all well-regulated colleges. We do not favor a game where brutality steps in and usurps the place of athletic development. It was simply a display of savagery which has tarnished the fair names of both schools."

He looked up once again. The crowd remained silent, anxiously awaiting his next words.

"I have a rebuttal, my friends," Herty offered. "You see, the evil is not in the game itself but in the shameful lack of appropriate facilities and training programs across the South, and most likely the nation. Instead of condemning sports, lawmakers should consider provisions for their proper development. I knew Von Gammon, and my regret over his death is genuine and sincere. But if Von were here with us today, God rest his soul, I wonder which side of the issue he would support?"

From their spot behind the assembly, J.A. embraced Rosalind as they shed tears together. Monty wrapped his long arms around both parents and held them snug against his chest.

Herty fielded a variety of questions from the press over the next fifteen minutes or so, and once the session came to an end, everyone began filing into the Capitol.

Thomas Reed entered the hallway and immediately spotted reporter Harry Hodgson, who was feuding with one of his staffers.

"No, you're not listening to me!" Harry argued. "I want tomorrow's headline to read, *THE END OF FOOTBALL*, with no question mark at the end. In fact, tell them no punctuation, period!"

The inexperienced correspondent nodded while scribbling on a notepad.

"Now get going, or we'll miss the deadline!"

Reed approached as the young man scurried off with his orders, "They are pushing this bill through way too fast, Harry."

"Fear is a great motivator, Thomas," the journalist proclaimed. "It would be political suicide for any of these representatives to vote against this measure right now."

"And that thought gnaws at me," Reed asserted. "Are we ready to ordain tiddlywinks and lawn tennis as our national games?"

A call rang out from inside the chamber. It was time for the vote.

* * *

All House Representatives were in their seats. The public viewing gallery and balcony were at maximum capacity. The chamber was abuzz with chatter.

But all talk ceased following the hammers of the gavel. The Speaker addressed the room, "I would like to call Representative John Slaton of Fulton County to the podium. He will speak on behalf of the anti-football bill."

Slaton thanked the Speaker as he took his place up front. He'd been informed that the Gammons were in attendance and located their position in the balcony. Out of courtesy, Slaton acknowledged J.A. and Rosalind with a smile and a nod before beginning.

"Thank you again, Mr. Speaker, and fellow members of the House. Over thc past two days, we have all heard various debates over the virtuous and malicious traits of football. I've seen but one game, but in that single afternoon, I became satisfied that football is too brutal. I was immediately outraged to hear that this senseless tragedy occurred in Fulton County, and am therefore a staunch supporter of this legislation. As lawmakers of this state, neither I nor any of you may favor an activity where so-called athleticism is nothing more than a bread and circus stunt that glosses over its savage cruelty and resulting heartbreak, such as this incident before us."

The Gammons continued to listen from up in the balcony.

"My colleagues, if we sit idly by and do nothing, that same savagery transcends us. We have an opportunity here today to make a progressive statement to the nation."

As a vast majority of cheers drowned out the few jeers, Monty leaned over to J.A. and whispered, "Except Dr. Herty, this discourse from Slaton is no different than everything else we've read or heard since arriving in Atlanta."

"Well, the incident did occur on his hometown soil, so perhaps he feels the need to . . ."

J.A. was cut off mid-sentence when Rosalind gawked her neck and shushed him. As soon as her attention was back on the podium, J.A. leaned back toward Monty and muttered, "It appears that *someone* is interested in what he . . ."

"I said SSSSHHHH! The both of you!" Rosalind yelped.

Having been scolded a second time, the two men looked toward the front of the chamber and pretended to listen with great interest.

The votes were cast shortly after, and the anti-football bill passed the House by an overwhelming 91-3 majority. Representative James Nevin of Floyd County, and therefore the city of Rome, was one of the few dissenters that voted against its passage.

Out in the hallways of the Capitol building, Governor Atkinson and his wife Susan had awaited the Gammons exit from the chamber. After an exchange of pleasantries, Mrs. Atkinson took Rosalind's hand and said, "I tell you, Rosalind, that football game on Saturday was the most barbaric display I have ever witnessed. Thank heavens there was plenty of support to move this bill along to the Senate."

In somewhat of a distracted stupor, Rosalind simply nodded her head and showed a polite smile.

Mrs. Atkinson scoffed, "You know, I find it quite ironic that the only people still favoring that horrible pastime are the ones who play it. They should be scared for their lives."

Awakened from her trance, Rosalind asked, "I am sorry, Mrs. Atkinson, but will you please come again?"

A quick smirk from the governess was followed by, "You understand, dear. The few players and trainers who came forward this week to defend football – why they all seem to be turning a blind eye toward the danger."

Rosalind quipped, "Yes, well, they love the sport. We call football a game, but they see something more than just the gridiron."

"Grid *what*?" Mrs. Atkinson sneered.

"Grid-iron," Rosalind pronounced in two syllables. "It's another name for the field that they play on."

"My word, honey," Mrs. Atkinson contended, "the name of their field even sounds savage."

"Von was interested in many sports, and not just football," Rosalind continued. "He was a champion cyclist and also enjoyed running track, playing baseball, boxing . . . you name it. If you stop and think about it, all of those things can be dangerous, too."

"Well, sweetie, once my husband signs this football bill, that will be one less thing for mothers to fret over."

Rosalind added, "In fact, two other boys from back home died in the past year; one while skating and another rock climbing, I believe." She snickered before, "You know, I don't recall such a fuss being made over abolishing those activities."

Confused over what she thought were odd statements for the situation, Mrs. Atkinson looked upon Rosalind with pity.

But Rosalind carried on, "Von had dreams of perhaps winning an Olympic gold medal someday. He strived to compete at the highest level, and I am glad that I was able to see him play for the Red and Black."

After having conversed off to the side, the governor and J.A. interrupted their wives' discussion.

"Again, please accept our deepest condolences for your loss, Mrs. Gammon," Atkinson offered. "Your family will continue to be in our prayers."

J.A. returned, "And thank you for your hospitality, Governor Atkinson. My dear wife does look exhausted. We've had little sleep since Saturday so please excuse us as we retire to our hotel."

"Of course, and I will make sure that a carriage arrives in the morning to bring you to our home for breakfast. Afterward, the Mrs. has scheduled a tour of our grand city for you all."

With a respectful expression and tone, J.A. declined, "Thank you, but no, Governor. We'll be boarding a train back to Rome early in the morning. Monty and Nellie need to get back to their little girl. She's being kept by a young lady back home, and we shouldn't burden her too long."

"Very well, but you have my confidence that this bill will soon pass the Senate. It will require nothing more than my signature after that," the Governor assured.

The Gammons expressed their gratitude again before parting company.

Once out of earshot, Mrs. Atkinson commented, "That poor, Rosalind. For a moment there it sounded as if she might be opposed to this measure."

Still smiling and waving to the Gammons, the governor replied, "You must have misinterpreted what she said, Susan. The game just took her boy's life, for Heaven's sake."

* * *

GAMMON HOTEL ROOM
LATER THAT NIGHT

Alone in the room, Rosalind sat before a roll top desk. It had not taken long to write down what she wanted to say. The words had flowed easily from head to pen to paper. She took more time reading and rereading her work looking for errors or potential revisions, but in the end, chose not to change a thing. Thinking about the governor's farewell remark earlier that day, Rosalind decided that the only thing needed to complete *this* particular document was *her* signature.

The deadbolt turned and the door opened. J.A. shivered as he came in from the chilly autumn evening.

"It's turned darn cold since the sun went down."

Rosalind remained seated with the transcript held against her chest, “How was dinner, dear?”

J.A. noticed her protecting whatever paper she had, but he chose not to mention it. Not yet, anyway.

“Quite disappointing, actually,” he reported. “You’d think a fancy hotel like this would bring your soup out when it’s hot. And not overcook your meat, either.” He held out something wrapped in a dinner napkin, “I know you said that you weren’t hungry, but they did have some marvelous cornbread.”

Rosalind tilted her head and smiled, “Thank you. Just put it on the table. I might nibble on it before bed.”

She turned her page upside down atop the desk. That move was so obvious that J.A. felt compelled to inquire about its secrecy.

“What are you hiding there, Rosie?”

With one protective hand on top of the paper, Rosalind replied, “John, you once acted like a silly boy upon the simple mention of football. Do you really want to see its extinction?”

“Well, I admit that I enjoy watching the game, but we are talking about life and death, here. Our *son’s* life and death.”

Looking down toward the floor, Rosalind recalled, “When Dr. Herty spoke on the Capitol steps, he mentioned something about Von’s opinion on the matter. I don’t remember the politicians ever asking or considering what Von would have wanted?” She looked up and straight at her husband, “Do you know who James Connolly is?”

“No, I don’t believe so,” he responded with a shrug. “Is he from Rome?”

“Oh, no matter. You wouldn’t understand.”

“You are right, Rosie. I *don’t* understand.” J.A. contended.

Rosalind questioned, "And how about us? Why, for as long as I can remember our house has been a playground for all the boys in Rome. Have you taken an inventory on the porch or inside the barn of late?"

"Well, as I recall there's a punching bag and gloves, two or three bicycles, several pairs of skates, a few tennis racquets, and balls for playing almost any sport."

"We even allowed our boys to play shinny down by the railroad, and not once did we fret over their safety," Rosalind testified. "I mean, how dangerous is shinny by the tracks?" she finished emphatically.

"What's your point, Ma?"

With her eyes now back on the carpet, Rosalind said softly, "He was such a good boy, John. Never smoked or spit tobacco. Never drank alcohol. Always turned in at a decent hour."

J.A. agreed to the character assessment with a nod of his head and a curious groan.

Rosalind looked back at him and continued, "Think how much he respected Emily. I know we raised him in the church, but I also believe his purity is a by-product of participation in sport, primarily football. That's exactly what Coach Warner touted when we first met him."

"Seems that you've become a football fanatic only *after* our son's tragic accident."

"No. I'm not a fanatic," Rosalind attested. "I've only now realized that football gave Von life in the first place. It was deeply important to him."

J.A. crossed his arms, "Well, I'll be. I can hardly believe what I am hearing. You should have spoken up sooner if you truly feel this way. Herty brought forth a strong argument, but they may have actually listened to you."

"I know that I should have, John." Rosalind lifted her hand from the paper and flipped it topside. "But no matter, I've penned a letter and I'd like it delivered to Mr. Nevin's office at the Capitol building tomorrow morning."

"That's not going to help any. His group already passed the thing, and now it's going to roll through the Senate like a freight train."

Rosalind countered, "Mr. Nevin was one of only three that voted against the bill. It seems he knew what Von would have wanted, meaning he shares the same opinion that bears heavy on my heart." She placed her face in her hands and said, "It makes no difference what the Senate does. I just need someone with access to the governor who can bend his ear before he takes a pen."

J.A. smirked and shook his head in disbelief. His reach toward Rosalind was an unspoken request to review the letter. She handed it over, and he read it silently.

After reading the final word, J.A. looked up and promised, "Alright, Rosie. I'll run it by his office in the morning on our way to the rail station."

Rosalind took the page back and signed the bottom:

*Yours most respectfully,*

*Von Gammon's mother*

# UPON FURTHER REVIEW

GAMMON HOUSEHOLD
FRIDAY, NOVEMBER 19, 1897

Despite the cloud cover and a chilly northern wind blowing outside, Will had played out in the yard with one of the neighbor boys, tossing and chasing a football around for hours.

Inside their home, J.A. sat comfortably in his wingback chair reading a newspaper. He waited for a break in the sounds of rattling dishes coming from the kitchen before hollering out.

"Rosie, come in here please!"

A tired Rosalind ambled into the parlor, still holding a rag and a bowl.

J.A. pointed to the front-page article and reported, "Says here the football bill passed the Georgia Senate yesterday by a count of thirty-one to four."

Rosalind's downtrodden expression remained unchanged.

"I suppose ninety-something to three in the House followed by this tally confirms how people truly feel about football," J.A. suggested as he looked at his wife.

Rosalind choked up, prompting J.A. to stand from his chair, put down the paper and hold her, tenderly.

"Oh, don't you fret, Ma," he started, "you have suffered too much anguish from all of this. Perhaps we should allow the passing of this law to provide us with some closure."

Fighting through tears, Rosalind admitted, "I am still confused over the matter, John. You know, which side to support. It's obvious that the vast majority of people oppose the game, but I keep coming back to the same conclusion; that Von would not agree with them."

She pushed far enough apart to gaze into her husband's eyes, "Would you think I'm crazy if I said that sometimes I hear Von's voice telling me how I should think about all of this?"

"No, dear, you're not crazy. In fact, out of everyone you've probably been the most level-headed person involved."

"Hopefully Mr. Nevin doesn't think I'm crazy, either," she thought. "I mean, he voted against the bill. But based on yesterday's outcome it doesn't appear that he had any success changing the opinions of his friends in the Senate; even after receiving my letter."

"Perhaps he never read your letter?" J.A. proposed. He took her by the chin and comforted, "Regardless, you know it matters not whether James Nevin even attempted to persuade members of the Senate. At present, there is still one person who can stop this bill from becoming law." He released her chin and kissed her on the forehead before, "I'll place a call to Mr. Nevin when I get into the store on Monday morning."

* * *

## GEORGIA CAPITOL BUILDING; OFFICE OF THE GOVERNOR TUESDAY, NOVEMBER 23, 1897

An animated congressional steward named Millard leaned his thin body around the door frame and rapped his knuckles against the trim work. Governor Atkinson, who'd been staring out his window, turned in his chair to address the caller.

"Hello, Millard. The door is open. Please, come in."

"Good morning, Governor," he greeted while taking a step inside the room. "Mr. Nevin has requested a meeting with you."

The governor was perplexed by the announcement. "Thanks for the warning, Millard," he replied sarcastically. "Schedule it on my calendar. Find something the week after next, will you?"

Millard stole a quick glimpse behind and then said in a high whisper, "But Mr. Nevin is standing in the hallway, sir. He is literally on the other side of this wall behind me, waiting to see you now."

Taking that as his cue, Nevin advanced into the room and approached the governor. Atkinson rose from his chair and stepped out from behind his desk. Millard darted back into the hallway and disappeared.

"Well, hello, James," the governor began as they met and shook hands in the middle of the room. "What seems to be so urgent? Heavens, it's only two days before Thanksgiving. There's scarcely a soul still at work here in the Capitol."

"Yes sir," James acknowledged, "and the slow down afforded us this opportunity to meet. I appreciate you making the time for me."

"But I haven't made any time?" Atkinson stated in the tone of a question. "Whatever you need to discuss can wait, am I right? I would prefer to have no new business on my plate before the turkey dinner. Heartburn, you understand," he finished with a fist pump to the chest.

"I would like to discuss the football bill, sir. Can we sit?"

The governor exhaled and reluctantly pointed to one of the high back chairs. They both took a seat.

"But that's *old* business, James," Atkinson reminded. "Over and done with. Your constituents back home should be very pleased, and when you return to Rome tomorrow for the long weekend, please assure everyone that I will sign the darn thing immediately upon my return from holiday. I suppose it's a bit ironic now that I think about it, but I've been distracted by that ordinance Mr. Mansfield recently introduced to legalize prizefighting and have inadvertently put off the football bill."

Nevin leaned forward in his chair, "Well, Governor, the speed in which you sign the measure is not what concerns me."

"Then what can I possibly do for you?"

Releasing a sigh of his own, Nevin requested, "I've come to ask for your veto, respectfully."

Initially, Atkinson figured the state representative was teasing. He stood on his feet, shaking his head and giggling aloud.

"You can't be serious," the governor insisted. "I know that you voted against it and appreciate your position, but frankly it's inconsequential. Every newspaper, parent, and educator within a thousand miles favors this bill. Why, you sat in the chamber with the rest of us and heard all those lectures regarding the evils of the dang sport. Or perhaps you weren't paying attention?" he mused.

Atkinson sat back down and in good humor accused, "That or you have lost your cotton-picking mind. Insanity would certainly explain your ballot."

Nevin was straight-faced and not playing around, "I assure you that I am of sound mind, Governor. And you are right, my voice may not mean anything to anyone at this juncture, but I've become privy to a revealing opinion from someone who *does* matter."

"Alright, I'll admit that I am intrigued," the governor said with a smirk. "But no matter what new information you have, do not expect me to veto this bill. There is simply no one of consequence whose support would sway the overwhelming public sentiment at this point."

"Oh, I beg to differ, sir."

Nevin pulled Rosalind's letter from out of his inside coat pocket and held it up for Atkinson to see, "This was placed on my desk the day following the House vote. Mrs. Gammon wrote it, and I must have read it a hundred times since then."

"If whatever she scribed is so important, why have you waited so long to come forward?"

James explained, "Well, the letter was addressed to me and her sentiment aligned with my own. But, seeing as I had already cast my vote, I felt there was little more I could do. Add the resounding outcome in the House and Senate, and I was convinced that presenting the note to you or anyone else was most likely a moot point."

"So, what made you change your mind, Mr. Nevin?"

"Yesterday, I received a call from John Gammon. Considering that he contacted me by telephone and not telegraph, I knew that it was a matter of urgency. Anyway, he was calling to ensure that I had delivered Rosalind's letter to you and was quite disappointed to hear that I had not."

Nevin reached across the space between them and handed it to him.

"Well, now I have."

With his eyes squarely assessing the congressman and not yet the letter, Atkinson fumbled around inside his jacket and removed his reading glasses. Once in hand, he perched them on his nose and read silently:

*Dear Mr. Nevin,*

*It would be the greatest favor to the family of Von Gammon if your influence could prevent his death from being used as an argument detrimental to the athletic cause and its advancement at the University. His love for the college, and his interest in all manly sports without which he deemed the highest type of manhood possible, is well known by his classmates and friends. It would be inexpressibly sad to have the cause he held so dear injured by his sacrifice. Grant me the right to request that his death should not be used to defeat the most cherished object of his life.*

*Yours most respectfully,*
*Von Gammon's mother*

With head up and glasses off, Atkinson stretched his neck and cracked his knuckles before mumbling, "To live is to war with the trolls."

"Excuse me, sir?"

Without a word, the governor stood. He folded the letter carefully and placed it inside his jacket along with his spectacles.

Nevin reacted by taking to his feet and begged, "Please tell me that you're not going to just bury that letter inside your pocket?"

"I agree that this is a rather extraordinary development," Atkinson conceded, "and I assure you that I will take Mrs. Gammon's appeal under advisement. But also understand that I will respectfully consider all other arguments that have been presented."

James implored, "Your Excellency, the boy's own mother wants the game to live on."

Atkinson snapped back, "And *we* are upon the Thanksgiving holiday, Mr. Nevin. I will take up the matter again upon my return."

"I trust you shall," James confided, "and I apologize for not presenting the letter sooner. I have been torn between what I believe is the right thing to do versus merely going along with the majority opinion."

"Ah, the life of a politician. Good day, James."

Nevin nodded, and following an awkward hesitation spun around and left the office.

* * *

*Some say that the pen is mightier than the sword. That phrase certainly applies here, but I'd say it was your unconditional love for our son and willingness to stand up for what you believed in that ultimately won the day.*

*Your follow up letter written directly to the governor, which was then widely published in papers throughout the region, most likely sealed the deal. In it, you expressed:*

***"You are confronted with the proposition whether the game is of such a character as should be prohibited by law in the interests of society. In answer, unquestionably, it is not. In the first place, the conditions necessary to its highest development are total abstinence from intoxicating and stimulating drinks as well as from tobacco, strict regard for proper diet and for all laws of health."***

*In an unexpected turn of events, Governor Atkinson granted your request and vetoed the anti-football bill on December 7th – despite a combined vote of 122-7 across the Georgia Legislature.*

*In his decision he wrote:*

*"**Football causes less deaths than hunting, boating, fishing, horseback riding, bathing, or bicycling. If we are to engage in legislation of this character now under discussion, the state should assume the position of parent and forbid all sports to boys. The government should not usurp all the authority of the parent, yet this legislation is a long stride in that direction.***

***It would be unfortunate to entirely suppress in our schools and colleges a game of so great value in the physical, moral, and intellectual development of boys and young men.**"*

NORTH ROME ATHLETIC PARK; ROME, GA
CHRISTMAS DAY, 1897

A group of young people gathered to play an impromptu football game at the park, and a sizeable number of spectators turned out to watch.

Those making up the two teams on the makeshift gridiron included members of Von's family, Red and Black teammates, fraternity brothers, and other friends from Rome. J.A. and Rosalind were joined on the sideline by Emily, Nellie, and the baby. Many of James Nevin's constituents made up the rest of the crowd, which stretched from one end of the field to the other.

Thomas Reed was there also, prancing up and down the sideline flailing his stick.

"Wasn't it a great suggestion by Walter to play this Christmas Day game in Von's honor?" J.A. asked his wife.

"Yes, dear. Walter is a wonderful friend and young man."

"And how much would Von have enjoyed this day?" J.A. inquired. "This pleasant weather suggests which side of the football debate our good Lord favors."

Out on the turf, Reynolds called his team into a huddle.

"Hey, Will, you'll play this down at quarterback," he directed. "We'll surprise them with a sweep to the left."

Nervously, Will asked, "Are you sure, Mr. Tick?"

"Yep, he's sure," Cow answered with a wink toward Tichenor. "Football is in your blood. Let's see what you can do."

Will swallowed and glanced at his mother to gauge her mood. She caught his glimpse and returned a lovely smile and blew a kiss in his direction. Emily beamed as well and took the opportunity to wave at him.

He stammered nervously, "Gosh, thanks Coach Cow . . . and Mr. Tick. I'll do my best!"

"Just take the ball and do whatever comes naturally," Reynolds advised.

From off-field, the Gammons watched as the two teams lined up for the next play. Rosalind was the first to notice her youngest boy assume the quarterback position. She quickly pointed this out to J.A.; her beautiful smile shone at its very best.

"Look, John, they've moved Will behind center!" she expressed with delight. "Oh, dear, he sure does look a lot like his brother."

"Yes, seems we've seen this before," J.A. commented. "But I don't think my eyes will ever become weary of it." He cupped his hands around his mouth and hollered, "Don't drop the ball, son!"

Rosalind laughed and crossed her fingers.

On the field, the ball was snapped to Will, and the play was underway. He faked a handoff to the halfback Tichenor and kept the ball under his arm, dashing toward the left side of the line.

Seeing the action unfold, the spectators cheered enthusiastically for the ball carrier. On defense, Monty gained a forward position in the direct path of the runner.

Will wiggled right. Will wiggled left. But he quickly realized that two or three of his steps were matched by just one from his tall and rangy brother. The two siblings fought off laughter as they tried to outmaneuver one another.

Finally, Will burst forward and somehow managed to squirt under or through Monty's outstretched arms. From there, he ran the entire length of the field for a touchdown. Exhausted, Monty dropped to the ground and watched his little brother score, all the while laughing joyfully.

The on-field antics amused the non-playing Gammons. J.A. turned from the action and caught Rosalind enjoy the moment. She soon noticed his stare and playfully withdrew her cheerful expression.

"No, don't stop," J.A. requested.

Puzzled by his ask, Rosalind looked up. Her stunning smile reappeared. J.A. pulled her close and kissed her passionately. So much so that the surrounding crowd rewarded the couple with rousing applause.

Both teams took positions for the ensuing kickoff, drawing everyone's attention back to the field, including the Gammons.

The onlookers went back to cheering and hollering.

Thomas Reed marched and waved his stick high and proud.

The ball was kicked.

* * *

FIRST PRESBYTERIAN CHURCH, ROME, GA.
WEDNESDAY, NOVEMBER 2, 1904

*So, my beloved Rosalind, after years of enduring nothing but heartbreak, yours could bear no more. The Lord called you home but one day following the seventh anniversary of Von's passing. You have simply experienced too much grief for one person to endure in a single lifetime, including the untimely and insufferable death of our littlest one, Will. For those present here today who may be unaware, it was four years ago that our youngest fell in front of an arriving train after playing a baseball game for Rome High over in Cartersville.*

*I for one cannot say why the Lord would allow our family to be subject to so much agony and sorrow, but I am also faithful in knowing that it is not our place to contend. I find solace in scripture, and in this case, the Apostle Paul reminds us in the Book of Romans that the sufferings of our life are not worth comparing with the glory that is to be revealed to us once in Heaven.*

*And today, that glory has been revealed to you, my precious Rosie. You are in the presence of our Lord and Savior, Jesus Christ, and also reunited with our sons. I can only imagine how happy you must be; sharing that beautiful smile with all of those who surround you.*

*Some time ago, I asked if someone in the future looked back on your life and asked how would you like to be remembered, what would you say? Your answer was quick and confident: that you'd like for people to know that although you strived to be kind and love others deeply, you were also one tough gal; resolved to stand up for what you believed in.*

*You wanted them to know that, just like your son, you had grit.*

# WHATEVER HAPPENED TO?

Georgia returned to play on the gridiron in the fall of 1898. They accomplished a 4-2 record that year under Coach McCarthy, his second and final season in Athens. He never coached organized ball after that and instead made his professional mark in other areas.

Around the start of the twentieth century, the 'Alumni Athletic Field' on the U of G campus was aptly renamed 'Herty Field' and continued to serve as home turf for the Red and Black until the dedication of 'Sanford Field' in 1911. In the 1940s, Herty Field became a parking lot until it was thankfully transformed into a beautiful green space in 1999, complete with a fountain and historical plaque, marking its significance.

Glenn 'Pop' Warner went on to coach college football for more than 40 legendary years, compiling over three-hundred victories and two national championships along the way. The Pop Warner Youth Football League is so named in his honor.

John Heisman is another famous coach in this story. I find it interesting that shortly after leaving Auburn he ended up at Georgia Tech for fifteen years. I suppose he had an affection for coaching some of Georgia's most contentious rivals. Heisman was later instrumental in developing the voting system that selects the best college football player in the country after each season, and the first winner was recognized in 1935. Heisman passed away before the '36 award was given and, well, the rest is history.

All I know about Walter Wynn is that he played on the Rome High School football team in 1895. He is sitting next to Von in the one team photo that I found, and so I assume they were friends. I also liked his name and therefore made him Von's best bud in the story.

Emily, her father Ira, and Jack Pierce are all fictional characters.

During the decade beginning 1910, Reynolds Tichenor was an assistant coach at Auburn. In later years he officiated college football and was a timekeeper at college basketball games while also practicing law in Atlanta. Tick died in 1935, reportedly of complications from an ailment that he'd originally contracted while officiating Georgia's 1929 game vs. Yale. That was the game that christened the newly constructed Sanford Stadium. The same one that my grandfather Papa attended as a freshman.

After his two years as an assistant coach under McCarthy, Rufus Ben 'Cow' Nalley was selected as the head man at Georgia Tech in 1899. That team ended its season with a record of 0-6-1, and his coaching career was over. Due to a serious illness, Cow was on his deathbed in November of 1902. Legend has it the last thing he heard was that Georgia had defeated Auburn earlier in the day; their first win in the series since he played on the team back in 1896. After that, Cow smiled and lost consciousness forever. He was 31 years old.

Monty served for several years as principal of the Rome City Schools. In addition to his undergraduate degree from Georgia, he earned a Master's Diploma from the Teacher's College at Columbia University and served a year as the National Executive Secretary of the Girls Scouts in 1916. He was the only one of Rosalind and J.A.'s three boys to live a full life, passing in 1953 at the age of 79.

J.A. died suddenly of a stroke on August 5, 1905, less than one year after Rosalind had passed away. They are buried under a magnolia tree along with Von, Monty, and Will in Rome's Myrtle Hill Cemetery.

On the morning of November 5th, 1921, school officials and surviving members from the Virginia team that played at Brisbane Park on that fateful day twenty-four years prior, presented a bronze plaque to the University of Georgia during a ceremony inside the campus Chapel.

On it, Von and Rosalind are symbolically displayed along with the phrases, "The Cause Shall Live in which His Life was Given," and, "A Mother's Strength Prevailed." This is believed to be the only recognition in the United States that commemorates a woman's contribution to the game of football. It hangs today in the Butts-Mehre athletic facility, located on the University of Georgia campus.

That afternoon the Georgia team, by then known as the Bulldogs, managed to avenge the 1897 loss and defeated the Cavaliers 21-0.

# BIBLIOGRAPHY

Within this Bibliography, I reference numerous historical sources used during the writing of this tale, and appreciate all of them. But there are four that I found myself going back to time and time again, and would like to give them special recognition.

I'll start with the book *The Ghosts of Herty Field*, by the late John F. Stegeman. It is an incredibly detailed account of the first twenty-five years of football at U of G, and recommend it to anyone interested in learning more about the early days of the Red and Black.

Toward the end of his book, Mr. Stegeman revealed his All-Quarter-Century Team (1891-1916) and awarded Von Gammon the position of Second-Team Fullback. He also recognized several of Von's teammates on this honorary squad.

Mr. Stegeman was a practicing MD in Athens for over fifty years. His father, H.G. Stegeman, served as the Dean of Men and Athletic Director at the University and also coached each of the four main sports at the same time while at Georgia.

I would also like to acknowledge George Battey for his invaluable, 'behind the scenes' accounts of the Gammon family and the city of Rome in his book, *The History of Rome and Floyd County*.

Thomas Reed was a notable character in my story and also provided fascinating information about the University in his life's work, *History of the University of Georgia.* First a student and then alumnus of UGA, he retired as the school's registrar in 1945. His book documents the on-goings in Athens from the school's early beginnings until the late 1940s and is over four-thousand pages in length. Thanks to the Hargrett Rare Book and Manuscript Library at the University and the GALILEO initiative, one can now access the pages of this historical manuscript online.

A big thank you goes to the staff at the Sara Hightower Regional Library in Rome, Georgia, who in the early days of my screenplay research took the time to photocopy and deliver a wealth of information upon request.

One of the items mailed to me was a magazine article entitled, *Letter to the Governor*, by Jerry D. Lewis. It is the most detailed account of Von Gammon's tragedy that I've read in less than three pages. I am not sure what magazine this article appeared in, nor when it was first published, but it is one of my favorite pieces.

---

## Print Sources:


- Stegeman, John F., *Ghosts of Herty Field,* University of Georgia Press, 1966; Brown Thrasher Book, 1997
- Battey, George Magruder, *The History of Rome and Floyd County,* Webb and Vary Company, 1922
- Reed, Thomas Walter, *History of the University of Georgia*, University of Georgia, 1949

- Lewis, Jerry D., *Letter to the Governor; A Georgia Mother Saves Football*, magazine article provided by the Sara Hightower Regional Library, publication date unknown
- Griffis, Julie, *Death 90 Years Ago Almost Killed Football*, Rome-News Tribune, Sunday, July 5, 1987; article provided by the Sara Hightower Regional Library
- McCain, Stacy, *She Lost Her Son, but Saved the Game He Loved*, Hometown Heroes, Special Collections, Burgett H. Mooney III (News Publishing Company. "Past Times"), July 1996; article provided by the Sara Hightower Regional Library
- Author unknown, *October and Football Recall Von Gammon's Tragic End*, Floyd County Herald, October 11, 1946; article provided by the Sara Hightower Regional Library
- *Princeton Alumni Weekly,* Volume 6, No. 2, October, 1905
- *The Pandora, Volume VIII,* Published by the Fraternities of The University of Georgia, Chas P. Byrd, Printer, May 1895
- Revsine, Dave, *The Opening Kickoff: The Tumultuous Birth of a Football Nation,* Lyons Press, 2014
- Schafer, Elizabeth D., *Auburn Football,* Arcadia Publishing, 2004
- Cordery, Stacy A., *Juliette Gordon Low: The Remarkable Founder of the Girls Scouts*, Penguin, 2013


---

## Digital Sources:


- https://digilab.libs.uga.edu/scl/exhibits/show/covered_with_glory/
- https://www.georgiaencyclopedia.org/articles/business-economy/charles-herty-1867-1938
- http://accheritage.blogspot.com/2010/02/20-february-1892-georgia-and-auburn.html
- https://en.wikipedia.org/wiki/Reynolds_Tichenor
- https://en.wikipedia.org/wiki/Rufus_B._Nalley

- https://en.wikipedia.org/wiki/Charles_McCarthy_(progressive)
- *The Great Train Wreck*, an online video presentation from the Georgia Tech Alumni, Living History Program: https://mediaspace.gatech.edu/media/The+Great+Train+Wreck/1_4x7emevz
- https://housing.uga.edu/site/about_timeline
- https://railga.com/oddend/streetrail/atlantastr.html
- https://en.wikipedia.org/wiki/List_of_baseball_parks_in_Atlanta
- https://www.tarheeltimes.com/schedulefootball-1896.aspx
- https://georgiahistory.com/marker-monday-herty-field/
- https://www.heisman.com/about-the-heisman/john-w-heisman/
- http://www.interment.net/data/us/ga/floyd/myrtle-hill-cemetery/records-e-g.htm

---

Made in the USA
Lexington, KY
29 September 2019